The Wheatstone Pond

By the same author

THE CALL AND OTHER STORIES
ECHOES OF WAR
FUTURETRACK 5
THE STONES OF MUNCASTER
  CATHEDRAL
URN BURIAL

Robert Westall

THE
WHEATSTONE
POND

VIKING

VIKING

Published by the Penguin Group
Penguin Books Ltd, 27 Wrights Lane, London W8 5TZ, England
Penguin Books USA Inc., 375 Hudson Street, New York, New York 10014, USA
Penguin Books Australia Ltd, Ringwood, Victoria, Australia
Penguin Books Canada Ltd, 10 Alcorn Avenue, Toronto, Ontario, Canada M4V 3B2
Penguin Books (NZ) Ltd, 182–190 Wairau Road, Auckland 10, New Zealand

Penguin Books Ltd, Registered Offices: Harmondsworth, Middlesex, England

First published 1993
1 3 5 7 9 10 8 6 4 2
First edition

Typeset by Datix International Limited, Bungay, Suffolk
Filmset in 13/15 Monophoto Garamond
Made and printed in England by Clays Ltd, St Ives plc

A CIP catalogue record for this book is available from the British Library

ISBN 0-670-84898-0

FOR PHILIPPA MILNES-SMITH.
HAPPY FUTURE CHILLS.

CHAPTER ONE

All London feels lonely after dark now. But few districts feel lonelier than Wheatstone. It's the size of the houses; and their grounds. Whereas Victorian businessmen set up their mistresses in the small neat terraces of St John's Wood, they built their own Gothic piles in neighbouring Wheatstone. Ugly London brick, embellished with all the turrets and pinnacles and *porte-cochères* their tormented Romantic hearts could desire. Fretted cast-iron balconies that rusted dangerously; gargoyles that grimaced and blackened through the great Victorian pea-soupers.

The servant problem, after the Second World War, was the houses' downfall. Their owners moved somewhere *bijou* in Hampstead or Highgate, leaving them to rot as bed-sitters. Later, the Thatcherite boom brought a feeble gentrification, one family to a floor; and Thatcherite service industries, vulnerable as poppies to the economic winds.

These uncertain newcomers coo about 'original features'. Desperate house-agents have learnt to stress stained glass and plaster cornices, rather than central heating and double glazing. But all the improvements are within. Outside, in the over-large gardens, the elaborate fountains stand cracked and dry, ornamental trees grow unchecked to darken the windows and, everywhere, the dark insidious rhododendrons gather strength to bury all in their shadowy silence. Massive wooden gates rot on their hinges, forever open; then collapse leaving mere gaps of thin, rutted, puddled gravel that lead to parking for a dozen cars where once flowers bloomed. Nobody walks in Wheatstone; grass grows up through the cracks in the pavement, beneath the tall, leaning garden walls. After dark you hear the sudden smash of milk-bottles, or the panicky run of some benighted woman's footsteps. Plenty of shadows for muggers and worse.

Why do I choose to live there? These uncertain people, with their uncertain money and uncertain dreams, are my livelihood. I prosper by making their dreams a little more real; I sell antiques, of a sort. Don't come to me for anything good. I have no sets of Georgian dining-chairs for five grand, or decent oil-paintings or Louis XIV commodes.

My commodes are Victorian; with chamber-pots inside. Polished with dark-tan boot-polish to hide the scratches made by long-dead invalids. People use them to stand TV sets on; but they are curiously keen to have the intact chamber-pot inside. The commodes look well alongside my Victorian coal-boxes (complete with shovel, but never the original shovel); my fly-blown Victorian mirrors that you can hardly see your face in; my horrible oleographs of lumpish cows up to their bellies in some unbelievable river, the once-prized possessions of some Victorian pavior or plumber.

Ugly trash, but beautifully polished, to hide the fact that the carcasses of my grandfather clocks, the backs of mirrors, the bottoms of drawers, are new. I am a creature of my time; economical with the truth. Which often makes me grumpy, because I am in love with the beautiful and true.

Like the girl, woman, who walked into my premises one late March afternoon in 1987. I felt a prick of interest, because she was so tall. Odd, but I cannot help respecting women according to their height. I can never take a woman under five feet three seriously. I can be friends with them, spoil them, indulge them, because to me they are no more than pets. Whereas a woman over five feet eight is half-way to being a goddess; until she proves otherwise.

A cruel man would have said this woman was all teeth and eyes. The tips of her upper teeth were always visible, even in repose. But when her wide mouth smiled in greeting, fleetingly, the teeth were perfect. As for the eyes, they seemed full of the grey brightness of the March sky she had just left outside. Beneath heavy eyelids, which I always take as a sign of a passionate nature. Only Rembrandt could have done justice to her bone-structure, so fine she might have been any age from thirty to fifty. Her hair was fashionably streaked, so I had to judge her age by her neck. No trace of crêpiness; just those two horizontal lines that come to women in their thirties. She still had a touching trace of gawkiness, a casual air of being a student, enhanced by the UC London scarf hanging inside her open pink anorak.

She touched my gilt clock appreciatively in passing, with long slender fingers. She went up in my estimation; it was the only half-decent thing I had in the shop. I watched the subtle play of expressions across her face, as fluent as wind across a lake on some idle afternoon. Faces like that carry lines early; but these were good lines. Intelligence, a kind of gay, cynical humour. If I might still use that much-abused word . . .

Her first words were a disappointment.

'The police are dragging the Wheatstone Pond. That girl's body has turned up. Three days.'

'Oh!' I had not had her down for that sort of ghoul. Besides, I had known the girl. She used to come into my shop sometimes. The papers said she was called Margie Duff. She'd been a shy little thing, but I'd liked her.

'They've got frogmen down. Looking for clues, I suppose.'

I just shrugged. She sensed my disappointment and hurried on.

'They're bringing up some interesting stuff, that has nothing to do with the murder. Old pop-bottles . . .'

I nodded dismissively. I had not yet sunk to selling old pop-bottles, glass-alleys and Hamiltons, like some I could mention. They fetch seven or eight quid each, but they're a lot of bother to get clean.

'Rusty prams . . . bicycles . . . even an old motorbike. The police don't seem to know what to do with them. They're just leaving them lying about. Some kids are starting to muck about with them. It seems a shame . . .'

'Jap bike, is it?' I still wasn't really interested.

'No, it's a Scott Flying Squirrel. Very much pre-War, I imagine.'

That got me going. Not just a woman knowing about Scott Flying Squirrels, which was strange enough, but the idea of kids mucking about with a classic or even vintage motorbike that, restored, might

4

be worth thousands. I twisted my shop-door sign round to read 'Back in fifteen minutes', locked up, and practically ran. 'She matched my pace easily.'

Wheatstone Park's a bit of a mess. They took the railings away for the War Effort in 1943, only to find they were unsuitable for munitions. So they dumped them in the shallows of the Thames Estuary, along with so many others. Just the gates remain, forever open, forever useless. The bigger trees still survive, and the inevitable rhododendrons. But there is little pleasure in walking there. Too many crushed Coke cans, contraceptives, syringes.

The Wheatstone Pond, from which our whole district gets its name, is about two acres, romantically irregular with one tiny wooded island. Well-escorted children still sail model boats there on Sunday mornings, but it isn't really satisfactory. The trees at the water's edge cause wind-shadows and sudden eddying gusts, so that a yacht will halt suddenly, for minutes on end, or change course without warning, as if steered by some ghostly hand. There is green scummy weed that rises from the depths to foul propellers. Beds of dead reed trap expensive plastic electric tugs and liners, far from the bank, where they bob and nod helplessly over the weeks while the sun bleaches their bright reds and blues to a sickly grey.

Around the Pond is a wide path of crumbling Tarmac, with sudden mini-cliffs to catch your feet and send you sprawling. Crowds gather there, spontaneously, on certain occasions after dark. I remembered one scene of sheer madness, one Guy Fawkes', when people had gathered to watch a distant firework display over Hampstead Heath.

Some fool had brought along, for a reason best known to himself, a beautiful scale model of a destroyer over three feet long. He put it into the water, and began to sail it, to the sound of ironic cheers. But then some other idiot threw a smoking firework at it. The firework floated upright in the water, the fuse still smouldering, like a cigarette-end in the dark. Then it went off, hurling a most realistic spout of white foam across the destroyer's bows. Like a miniature depth-charge. In a second, the crowd, which had merely been amiably drunken before, went into a frenzy. Suddenly, everyone was throwing fireworks at the destroyer. It vanished into a forest of waterspouts. One firework must have exploded on the deck, blowing the foremast and the radio-control away, for the destroyer began sailing in huge circles, while its frantic owner began attacking the firework-throwers at random.

But there were too many of them, and in the end the little vessel sank by the stern, its bow at last vanishing to a hysterical storm of cheering. A lovely model, made of sheet metal; thousands of hours of work.

I have disliked the Wheatstone Pond ever since.

By the time we got there, it was all over. Even the crowd of expressionless ghouls were starting to break up and drift away. The young police frogmen were packing up and laughing among themselves in that heartless way. A couple of wetsuits, one orange, one fluorescent green, were hanging like flattened corpses from the roof-rack of the police personnel-carrier.

The products of their search lay straggled along the crumbling path. Two ancient prams, five bicycles, and the motorbike. I walked across to inspect it. Three kids who had been spitefully twisting at its levers gave way very grudgingly. Its spokes were as thick as sausages with green slime. Banners of weed trailed from the handlebars. On the saddle the slime was drying and cracking and lifting already, in the bleak sunlight and sharp March wind. Some reluctant hand had smarmed the slime away from the petrol tank to expose the insignia. Probably my woman.

It was a Scott Flying Squirrel all right. And more nineteen-twenties than nineteen-thirties. I gave it sharp pokes, in places where I would have expected it to rust away. I'll never forget the smell of it: deep, dark, vegetable and oddly *alive*.

'Hardly seems to have rusted at all, does it, sir?' The voice of authority came over my shoulder. I straightened up. It was the Inspector in charge of the diving team. He wore one of their yellow waterproof jackets, with badges of rank, but he didn't look much like a policeman otherwise, with his thick grey polo-neck sweater and muddy wellies. There was a yellow waterproof stop-watch round his neck on a cord. He had steady calm grey eyes, with a possibility of a grin in them, and a brown weathered face. You could have taken him for a tugboat skipper.

'No, no rust. Odd!' I agreed.

'Probably lack of oxygen in the water. Nasty pond, this. Never like coming here. Slime must be God knows how many feet thick, down there. I shall be glad to get my lads out of it.'

'You're not . . . going on, then?' I looked down into the dark water and could hardly repress a shudder.

7

'No point. They've done the preliminary autopsy. No external signs of violence. Another suicide, they reckon. That's seven here, in the five years I've been doing this. Though why they choose *this* place . . .' It was his turn to repress a shudder.

'What happens to all this stuff?' I asked, to change the subject, indicating the motorbike.

'Awkward.' He sighed. 'We're a scratch team, drawn from all over the Met. All these lads'll be back on their own beats tomorrow. All we want is to get our gear stowed and get home. By rights this stuff should go down to the local nick, as lost property; but who wants the paperwork? Who wants the *stuff*, come to that? We had them look up the bike's registration on the Swansea computer. No sign of it. Reckon the thing's been here since the twenties. You wouldn't care to take charge of it, sir? You seem to know something about bikes.'

He looked at me hopefully, and added, 'We usually just leave the stuff, and it vanishes by the next morning. You know what people are. But it's usually smaller stuff . . . this could cause trouble if the kids get to it . . . I think there's still petrol in the tank . . . petrol or water.'

'I could cope with it,' I said. 'But it's a matter of proving provenance – I'm an antique dealer.'

His face brightened. 'You could always put people on to me, sir. I'll tell them where it came from. Here's my card . . . I'll put my home number on the back . . .'

'I'll fetch my Volvo estate . . . I could do with a hand . . . loading.'

'We'll be here ten minutes yet . . . hey, steady with that bottle, Harrison. Any bottles you don't want,

8

throw back in the lake. We don't want broken glass.' He turned back to me. 'Very keen on old bottles, the lads are. Got wonderful collections in the lounge at home, some of them. I think its the only reason they volunteer for the work.'

I was back in five minutes with the Volvo. They helped me load up willingly enough. I took two of the old push-bikes as well – ladies' models with curved crossbars and twenty-eight-inch wheels, and baskets fore and aft. There's a growing market for really old bikes now.

I gave them a twenty quid note for their trouble saying, 'Police Benevolent Fund, if you can't find a better use for it.' From their grins, I reckon it vanished down the till of their favourite pub. And who's to blame them?

The lady who'd started it all was still picking through the stuff on the path. I offered her a lift back to the shop. I reckoned, the way things had worked out, she'd earned herself a drink too. She stood up, delicately holding a shapeless lump of slime, about two feet long.

'I'll shove that in the back with the rest,' I said.

'Just as long as you don't drive off with it.'

'What is it?'

'I'm not saying. But I think I'm about to break your heart, Mr Morgan . . .'

'How do you know my name?'

'It's over your shop, silly.'

'Suit yourself.' I didn't reckon she could break my heart that day. Not with that Scott Flying Squirrel in the back, and a couple of bikes worth a hundred each, and all for twenty quid.

Which just proves how wrong you can be. She caused me heart-breaks all the way, that lady. Smart as a whip, and whips cause trouble.

CHAPTER TWO

I drove into the cobbled stable-yard behind my shop.
James and Lenny were waiting on tenterhooks;
there's always excitement with a big new find. My
blokes are not nine-to-fivers; sometimes, if there's a
rush, they'll work the whole weekend. Even James,
who's a Methodist lay preacher; though he'll take two
hours off to lay down the law in some pulpit, on the
Sunday. James loves putting the fear of God into
people.

We manhandled the motorbike off on to an old
waterproof mattress, by the central drain, and Lenny
put on his big rubber apron and wellies, and got the
pressure-hose on it. It was a pleasure to watch him
cutting through that slime.

'She's in fair nick,' said James. 'Look at that chrome
coming up on those handlebars. 'Course, chrome was
chrome in them days – chrome on brass – not like
modern rubbish.' We continued to watch the slow
resurrection in silence: the cream, red and gold of the
long, flat petrol-tank; the dark shine of the broad
saddle.

'Real leather, that. Hasn't rotted,' said James. He
shouted, 'That'll do, Len. That black stuff's oil – we
don't want that shifted yet.' Then he was in, trying
gently to move the wheels round, testing the links of
the drive-chain. ''Sa bloody miracle. Hardly a spot of

rust.' He hauled the bike upright and tried gently to push down the kick-starter. It moved quite easily. There was a low suck and sob, as if the engine wanted to fire. He put the bike on the rest and came back to us.

'Front forks are a bit bent – that'll be when it hit the kerbing afore it went into the water. Feller musta still been on it, crazy bastard. Bet that cooled his courage . . .' He looked at me. 'I think we'd better get her stripped down right away, and into the oil-bath. Don't want rust starting now. She musta been nearly new when she went in . . . Overtime be all right?'

He worships Mammon, does James, as well as God.

I nodded. The price that bike would fetch at Sotheby's . . . pity they have vintage sales so seldom, and take so long to pay out afterwards . . .

I turned to my guest. 'I'm very grateful for your tip-off. Those kids would've wrecked it. Can I offer you a drink?'

'I'd rather have a sink.' She held up the long sausage of slime she'd rescued from the back of my Volvo.

'Your every wish . . .' I led the way into the workshop. It's a huge shed of corrugated asbestos that somebody erected in the back garden during the War, before town planners were thought of, or neighbours complained. It's the reason I bought the place. One of the things I'd installed since was a long row of Belfast sinks. Amazing how often you restore an antique by soaking it in something. Stripper, acid, cat's-piss.

She couldn't have been less like our pressure-hose. She filled the sink and dunked the slimy sausage in gently, stroking away the weed with long fingers, pale green under the water. A patch of bright red appeared;

then a square inch of transparent celluloid, a tiny steering-wheel. A model car? Too long . . . Then a sharp bow . . . a model boat, a speedboat, and quite a big one. A hatch-cover with a hole for a winding-key. Another cockpit aft, with another windscreen.

'Oh, you jammy sod!' I said. 'A Hornby speedboat. Pre-War.'

'Number four,' she said. 'The one with two cockpits. It's one of the rarest . . .'

'D'you want to sell it?'

'No, Mr Morgan, I want to *keep* it. Put it on my mantelpiece and gloat over it.'

'Be a good investment,' I said grudgingly. 'Tin-plate toys are going up like a rocket.'

'There is more to this life than money, Mr Morgan.'

'Not a dealer, then?' She puzzled me. She knew a lot more than your average layman, who knows a bit more than your average laywoman, who can't tell a Mamod steam-engine from a whatnot.

'I'm at the City Toy Museum. Press and Schools Liaison, till I can get something better. I'll take that drink now.' She looked down at the clean but dripping boat, holding it away from her clothes.

'You'd better let James have that,' I said. 'He might be able to save the clockwork. Rust up solid, otherwise.'

She nodded, and gave it to me; a bit reluctantly, I thought. It's terrible, the reputation dealers have got . . . I don't really know why, but the public think we're all crooks.

I gave her a drink in the office where I deal with clients. We sat each side of the desk where I count out the fifty-pound notes, crumpling every one to make sure there aren't two stuck together.

13

'Interesting place, that Wheatstone Pond.' She crossed her legs; frowning about something else entirely. I liked her for that: her legs were so long and elegant that any other woman would have made a Trooping of the Colour of it. I dragged my mind back into the world of common sense.

'Pond's eighteenth century, latish, I reckon. Wheatstone Park used to be the grounds of a stately home . . . the last of the DeStaber family gave it to the public. Shame it's got so knocked about . . .'

'Curious, the way things don't rust . . .'

'Lack of oxygen . . .'

'There's not much oxygen where the *Titanic* is. But *she's* still rusted . . .'

'Well, it's our good fortune . . .' I steered away from the topic; she obviously knew a great deal more about it than I did.

'It makes you wonder what else might be down there, from the last two hundred years. Be a wonderful place for an archaeological dig. A lot more exciting than the middens round Jack Straw's Castle . . .'

'*I* don't fancy putting on a wetsuit and having a grope round down there. Not for all the Hornby speedboats in China . . .'

'But think of it. How many children must have sailed their boats there, in the old days? And how many must have sunk? You could make a whole history of model boats . . .'

'For the City Toy Museum?' I smiled a little. Everybody has an angle, everybody's on the make. It's just that some people are more subtle about it than others . . .

'Yes. Why not?' Her huge grey eyes were suddenly

challenging. 'It's been done once before. When the council cleaned out the Round Pond at Kensington, I think.'

'I can't see *this* council spending money cleaning out ponds. They can't afford to clean the streets, for fear of being rate-capped. And even if they pumped the Pond dry . . . that slime would be a death-trap till it dried out.'

'Oh, there are ways and means . . .'

'Everybody's got to have a dream,' I said, putting on my fake American accent. 'Meanwhile, another drink?'

'Just because you can't stop staring at a woman's legs doesn't make *her* into a fool.'

'Ouch. Can I take you out to dinner, to make up?'

'Only if you promise not to keep staring at my legs.'

'What part am I allowed to stare at, then?'

'My lips. If you're deaf and a lip-reader.'

By the time I saw her again, the Scott Flying Squirrel was restored and ready to go to its buyer. James said he'd never had an easier job. The mechanical side was a push-over; even the piston-rings were hardly worn, and the black layers of oil had kept everything shiny-new. The primitive electricals had to be replaced, but he found some new wire that looked like the old wire. He had most bother with the saddle; he had to dry it out very slowly, so it didn't crack and go iron-hard. It would never be a saddle for riding on again; but that was the new owner's worry. A young man with more money than sense, but that was before quite a lot of it vanished into my bank account. I hadn't bothered to wait for Sotheby's; just passed the word around the right people. Why pay Sotheby's commission? And their damned buyer's premium, which the seller really pays anyway?

She was patient with us. Waited while James kicked the bike into life; listened to the antique, long-lost chug of the single-cylinder engine with at least the appearance of interest. Then James presented her with her little speedboat, and she listened to the whirr of the clockwork, and watched the tiny propeller going round with much more interest.

'If you ever do sell it . . .' I said.

'Yes, you can have first refusal.'

As we settled over the prawn cocktails she said, 'You seen the local papers recently? The fuss at the inquest on Margie Duff?'

'You mean, the proposal to fill the Pond in?'

'Yes. I wrote to the coroner. As a concerned rate-payer. And the police like the idea . . . no more suicides.'

'Cost the earth to fill in.'

'On the contrary. It could make the council a bit of money. Controlled tipping of builder's rubble. Tipping space is at a premium . . .'

'What good will that do you? All your precious boats under a thousand tons of broken brick . . .'

'It would have to be drained first. And then we might get three months to do a rescue dig.'

'What'll you do for money?'

'Do it during the long vac; using local students who can't get a vac job, and are bored out of their minds. Living locally, we wouldn't even have to pay them a lodging allowance. A lot would do it just for the fun . . .'

'You jammy sod . . .'

She laughed. 'Our only problem is we'll have no-where to store the finds and work on them . . .' Her great grey eyes were on me. They were peculiarly hard to resist. It was partly her . . . physical frailty. She always looked as if a puff of wind would blow her away. Not an unhealthy frailty . . . but could ankles be so slender without breaking, wrists be so slender yet still have enough strength to take a screw-top off a jar of olives? If Marilyn Monroe was the Eternal Mistress, this girl was the Eternal Daughter, crying out to be cherished, delighted, protected. I'd seen the grin on even old James's face, when he gave her the speedboat. She must have spent her life being spoilt rotten. She was bringing out the father in *me*, and I couldn't have been ten years older than her.

But her mind was far from frail. 'Of course, *we* would only be interested in *toys*. Model boats, mainly. But anything else we found . . . after we'd examined it, we'd have no further use for it . . . I suppose we'd just leave it lying in the storage space, when we packed up and went . . .'

'That's *wicked*,' I said. '*Really* wicked. You could go to hell for things like that.' Of course I said it with a grin; but it was to haunt me later.

'You have got an awful lot of space in that work-shop of yours, Mr Morgan. And you did get quite a lot for that motorbike I put your way. I do think you owe us one . . .'

'You'd better call me Jeff, if we're going to be partners in crime . . .'

'Hermione,' she said. 'Here's my card. I've put my home number on the back.' She held out a slender hand. 'Shall we shake on it?'

I was so keen to get hold of that hand that I didn't read the card till later. The hand was smooth and cool and dry, and warned me not to squeeze it too hard. Then it escaped as swiftly as a bird, and she sat there primly eating her prawn cocktail, as if butter wouldn't melt in her mouth. I felt then she was a bit like a beautiful ghost, that had barely solidified into reality, and might dissolve away at any moment if you tried to get your arms round her. Men would desire her, and then find themselves unable to touch her.

Keats didn't live far from where we were eating. Keats's House is in Hampstead. And wasn't it Keats who wrote 'La Belle Dame sans Merci'? I only remembered one line of it, clod that I am.

'The sedge is withered by the lake, and no birds sing.'

I suppose I should have been warned then. I should, clod that I am, have lumbered back to my harmless faking and making of money. God knew, I'd had enough women in my short life. Plump, warm women, honest women, easy women. But the one you really want is the one you can't have.

Mind you, I had her mind. She gave very generously of her mind. She'd been to so many places I'd never thought about. Nowhere obvious, like Spain or even Provence. She'd been to the real *Hôtel du Lac*, and knew a couple of spicy titbits about the famous authoress herself; was uproariously funny about spending Up Helly Aa in Shetland; the German spas; grew indignant about the Government's neglect of Ascension Island.

But you could never have accused her of showing off, for such ludicrous disasters had befallen her in every place, making her out to be such a hopeless fool, that she quite disarmed you. I confess I spent a very enjoyable evening; one of the most enjoyable evenings of my life.

At her door, she offered me one smooth slim cheek before an awkward silence could develop. Then she was gone, before I could expect to be asked in.

That smooth cheek grew very familiar, over the months that followed!

I didn't like it when the policemen came into my shop, several weeks later. Policemen make me nervous, especially when they're in uniform. Somebody sees them, and suddenly the gossip is all round the world of London dealers. I'm being charged at Bow Street with receiving the Crown Jewels. Or the VAT man has finally caught up with me. It's very bad for trade.

'Yes, sergeant?' I said, my voice very sharp. I knew I wasn't in any real trouble. For one thing, I hadn't done anything, and for another, I could see that their car was a traffic car.

'I believe you sold a motorbike recently, sir? BCM 120?'

'Yes,' I said wearily, wondering who had made the allegations. And wondering, too, if that Inspector with the police diving team would be as good as his word and look after me.

'In your estimation, sir, was it in roadworthy condition when you sold it?'

'It had passed its MOT,' I said, with a little heat. We had taken real pride in its passing its MOT. 'But of course, it was a very old bike. I mean, it didn't have disc brakes. It wouldn't have had the cornering ability of a modern bike. It wasn't really sold for riding on. Not every day.'

'Not meant for riding on every day,' said the sergeant heavily, and it was like an accusation. He made a note in his notebook.

'What I mean is that it was an antique. Quite a rare and valuable antique. Only a fool would ride it every day. But a little spin round the arena of a vintage car rally would be OK. I mean, a serious owner wouldn't want to wear it out – wear away its *value* . . .'

'A little spin at a vintage car rally,' said the sergeant, and wrote something else in his notebook. 'You warned the purchaser of these facts when he purchased, did you, sir?'

'Yes, I did. But I mean, he knew. He knew what he was buying. You wouldn't pay that kind of money for a second-hand Japanese banger . . .'

The sergeant glanced round. 'You're not . . . you don't deal in second-hand bikes normally, sir? Not as a regular thing?'

'I'm an antique dealer, sergeant. I sell *antiques*. I am not a garage. That bike was sold as an *antique*. What the hell is all this about? Why can't you ask the owner this sort of stuff? Has he complained?'

'He's not likely to do that, sir. He's dead. Broken neck. Went out on the bike you sold him at half-past three in the morning. Took a corner in a way that would have taxed a modern bike. Seventy he was doing, they reckon.'

'Drunk,' I said bitterly. Thinking about all the trouble we'd taken with that bike. And now it would be a heap of junk. Something unique wasted – by a crazy young pup with more money than sense.

'No, sir,' said the sergeant heavily. 'As a matter of fact the coroner recorded he was stone-cold sober. All he had in his stomach was the remains of a meat pie.'

CHAPTER THREE

'Well, wotcher think?' asked James, patting the Regency side-table as if it was his prize pig. 'Which legs is which?'

I examined the piece carefully. I'd paid five quid for it at an auction held at a sports centre in Pinner. Beautiful walnut top, with crisply moulded edges. But when I bought it, there had only been two legs and a snapped-off stump. Some fool had sat his fat backside on one end and . . . bingo.

I examined the four legs. The turning on the two new ones was as exquisite as the original; James was a genius with the lathe. Tiny blemishes on all four legs, where the feet of ages had kicked them. The soft patina of polish was the same, and the colour . . .

'The back legs are the fakes,' I said to James.

'Why?' he demanded indignantly.

'Because only a fool would put the fakes to the front where they'd be noticed.'

'Well, that's where you're wrong. That's what any fool of a dealer would think. They'd examine the back legs extra careful, so I put the replacements on the *front*.' He sniffed in wicked and righteous triumph. 'The colour was hell to match. Know how I got it? Three layers of black coffee, one of lemon juice and Worcester sauce; mixed. Just right, innit?'

I must explain about James. He is an interesting

case. To look at, he is the soul of nonconformist righteousness. Silver hair, short-back-and-sides. Six feet three and a back like a ramrod. A red-veined drinker's nose, red-veined drinker's cheeks, even red-veined drinker's ears. Which is unfair, because he never touches a drop. He blames it on his indigestion. In his more relaxed moments, he jokes that he cannot stomach this wicked world. Preaches twice most Sundays, going out in his old Humber as far off as Ealing, where the congregation never numbers more than twelve. Preaches hell-fire. Doesn't want much mercy on earth for sinners either. Wants to bring back hanging, and not just for murder. For adultery too. People think he's winding them up at first. Their kind, liberal faces when they realize he's serious . . .

But in the matter of restoring antiques, he's the best liar in the business. He says he learnt all he knows in Italy, in 1945. The soldiers hadn't a lot to do, once the War finished. But he found a little Italian who was making a good living gathering brass off the battle-fields – cartridge-cases, shell-cases – and melting it down to fake small classical statues. And ageing them a lovely green by burying them for a month in the urine-sodden straw from cow-byres . . . he reckoned that Italian's work was still on view in the V. & A. to this day.

How he equated the tricks he pulled on antiques with his religion, I could never quite work out. Except that we sold, not to the rich, exactly, but not to the poor either. And he never ceased to rail against the habits of our Wheatstone rich; the wife-swapping, which he still maintained went on in our local wine-bar (though why he was so certain I have never been able to find out); the divorces and remarriages so that some men could boast three wives and ten kids; the teenage sex of the latchkey kids who came home from the comprehensive at lunch-time to make love in comfort in their parents' beds . . . there was no point in arguing with him, because once started he could go on for hours. Of my good working-time.

I had tried sharing my unease with him, about the young man who had died on our motorbike. All he could find to say was that what he had been doing *must* have been wicked, simply because he was doing it at half-past three in the morning, a time when God-fearing people had been in their beds and asleep for hours.

He had even vouchsafed an unhealthy interest in the wreck of the bike. If we could get it back, perhaps we could restore it again for another good profit . . . He gave me a look of utter contempt when I shuddered and closed the subject. But I wasn't having anything to do with death-bikes.

And it still worried me, in quiet moments. If we had not saved that bike, the young man would be alive still. Maybe there was something we had missed . . . that even the police vehicle-examiners had missed. I'd never killed anybody before – it's quite different from swindling someone.

Just then, young Lenny came in, wild as a kid with excitement, to say they'd started pumping out the Wheatstone Pond. There was an appliance from the local fire brigade up there now, and the water they were pumping out was running past our very door. We all went out, to inspect the novelty. Wheatstone Park is uphill from us, and our gutter was flooding

24

five or six inches deep, with little pools forming on the pavement. It reminded me of those French towns, where they sluice the gutters every morning, to clear away the litter. Except it wasn't so pleasant. The water from the Wheatstone was black and opaque, and it smelt vile. I wondered how far it would run downhill; but it wasn't running far. Every drain-cover was sucking it in. A hundred yards on it was no more than a trickle. We have good drainage on that slope.

We wandered up to view the proceedings. The firemen seemed to be enjoying themselves, but they had to stop every so often, to clear the dense masses of green slime out of their filters. And the Wheatstone seemed as full as ever.

By lunch-time, though, it was four inches down, and by tea-time, a good foot. The reed-beds were drained, the bottom of their stalks fattened to an inch with slime, and the poor trapped bobbing plastic boats were stranded. And some watching urchins were starting to go after them, stepping out gingerly, holding each other's hands in lengthening lines.

We were just turning away, back to work, when there was a sudden scream and flurry, about fifty yards away. We turned to see one of the chains of boys scrambling ashore. The last one in the chain was black with mud up to his knees ... serve the little sods right.

And then I saw with horror that that boy had not been the last in the chain. One boy had been left behind.

I had not noticed him at first, because he was already up to his chest in the black slime. All you could see was his frantically waving arms and bobbing head, which did not look quite human.

I think we all ran. All gazed in horror at that milk-white face, with its staring eyes, and the lapping black water reaching up for the mouth; at the way the head strained upwards, to avoid the little waves, and in doing so, sank another perceptible inch. It was the child's look of disbelief, as he stared at us standing in perfect safety only yards away . . .

It was lucky that the fire-crew were better men than we were. There was a rattle of aluminium ladders, a fireman crawling with a rope tied to the back of his belt. Another fireman joining him on the other side. They lifted the child a little, so his muddy gaping mouth was pulled clear. And then we all took a hand on the ropes, and pulled like men possessed when we were told to. And, with a loud sucking noise, he was safe, just screaming with terror.

It was then I realized the Wheatstone Pond was a real killer.

By evening, it was imprisoned behind twisting police tapes and hurriedly-painted warning notices. But it still killed a venturesome Alsatian that night. And would have had the owner too, if he had not been held back, sobbing, by passers-by.

There was a hell of a fuss in the local paper. Some idiots suggesting that the Wheatstone be filled in immediately, before it was even drained. There were women with petitions, going from house to house. For a week, we really became the community we never had been. People talked to strangers in the street, and all about the Wheatstone Pond. And then about the Wheatstone stink. Because, as more and more of the slime was exposed, bubbling and plopping evilly under the early

May sun, that peculiar dark *living* smell crept in through every warped and ill-fitting Victorian window.

But all the fuss, and all the petitions were to no avail. The council said the Pond must be allowed to drain properly before tipping began. Water would be seeping into it from the hillside above, though no one knew how or where yet. Until these water-sources were located and culverted, there was a risk that the whole Park might turn into one uncontrollable swamp, and the forced-out slime might start flowing downhill, to where most of us lived. Blocking the surface-drainage; perhaps even blocking the sewers. . . . It was enough to silence the petitioners. We were offered the choice, even, to go back to the Pond as it had been. But there was no going back. Everyone hated it too much by now. Everyone wanted it turned into a nice safe playing-field or tennis-courts . . .

Meanwhile, under the ministrations of the increasingly bored and fed-up fire brigade, the level of the water sank and sank. The weather continued warm, and the margins began to dry out and crack. And Hermione appeared with her first volunteers and a lorry full of wooden industrial pallets and ladders. Lenny, who seemed more fascinated by the Pond than anybody else, came running back in the lunch-hour to tell us. I strolled up there.

A crowd had gathered, of course. Early-retired men, with newspapers under their arm and dogs firmly on a leash. School truants, keeping a wary eye out for curious policemen. And the local female vigilantes, who saw the Pond as a lasting threat to their offspring, and were ready to ring the local paper and howl blue murder at the least provocation.

'God,' I said. 'How can you ever hope to find anything in *that* mess?'

She pointed at the wide saucer-shaped glistening surface of the mud. 'Don't you notice anything?'

'Nope!'

'Little mounds appearing on the surface? Well, as the mud dries out and shrinks, the objects trapped in it don't. They stick up more and more day by day. We're going to dig out the mounds.'

I eyed the mounds with disgust. 'They look like little graves . . .'

'Archaeologists like graves. Where do you think they got Tutankhamun from?' She left me, and went forward to supervise. Watching, it did seem to me she knew pretty well what she was doing. The first pallet, three feet square and six inches deep, was flung out over the mud with a swing and a cheer. A builder's ladder was lowered out on to it. The smallest of the students, a girl with long dark hair, stepped on to the ladder. She wore wellies, and had a rope tied round her waist. The pallet sank to half its depth, then stopped. She waved from it, and returned to shore. Two male students carried a second pallet out along the ladder, and, by delicate manoeuvring, placed it on top of the first, which by this time had almost vanished in the ooze. And this second pallet stayed clear, on the surface. Then another pallet was heaved out from the safe platform. They grew so accomplished, it became boring, and all the ghouls, who had been waiting for another disaster, packed up and went home. And I went back to work and sold a three-piece Victorian bedroom suite in mahogany. I was still counting the notes when there were excited voices in the yard out back, and I knew the first discovery had arrived. I ran to see as avidly as anybody else.

Into the Belfast sink it went. Again, those long slender hands teased and pulled at the encrusted slime.

Three inches of shiny grey tin plate, with black lines on it. The tip of a mast . . . a tripod mast . . . a warship mast. My heart was in my mouth. One tip of a funnel, another, another, a fourth. The second mast. A gun-turret, a propeller . . .

Hermione raised it up at last, dripping, shining, as a footballer might have raised the FA Cup. Perfect in every detail, the little lead sailors even, raising telescopes to their eyes, or signalling with bright flags. Two feet long.

'You know what it is, Morgan?' She didn't even try to keep the triumph out of her voice.

'German tin plate. An armoured cruiser. Probably about 1898. Clockwork motor . . .'

'Probably by Marklin.' She would have to have the last word. 'Probably fetch two thousand at auction, in this condition, wouldn't you say?'

'Probably more,' I admitted. All the students cheered like mad. 'You'd better hand it over to James. We don't want it . . . going rusty . . .'

She thrust it into my hands, still leaking water, and in a second they were all running back to the Pond, shouting and laughing. I suddenly wanted to go with them. It was a bit like I imagine a gold-rush might have been, in the nineteenth century. When whole ship's crews jumped ship and headed for the Klondike, or Ballarat. Infectious, catching.

To everyone but James. He examined the little cruiser with a searching critical eye, looking for faults.

Then he pointed to the propeller, which was slightly bent askew.

'Knocked the propeller, opened up the stern-gland, let in the water and down she went. I'll bet some spoilt brat went to bed crying *that* night. Though I expect his rich daddy bought him another one straight away.' He sniffed, and said, 'I'll get it in the oil-bath, afore they bring down any more. I hope you've got plenty of insurance cover.'

I found it impossible to concentrate on selling antiques. Every time I heard a noise in the yard, I just had to go through. I even abandoned a man who was contemplating buying a Viennese wall-clock for five and a half. After five minutes he followed me into the shed and grumpily began thrusting notes into my hand. But the moment he saw the excitement round the Belfast sink, he could not resist joining in as well.

This time it was a small bundle of cloth. With shaking fingers, Hermione undid the knots . . .

An old blue linen shirt, wrapped round . . .

The revolver glistened eerily; blue highlights on black steel. I took it off her.

'An Enfield .45,' I said. I broke it, to expose the revolving cylinder, with its cartridges. 'Two shots fired.'

Hermione and I looked at each other. I think the same thought came to us simultaneously. I said, 'I think you'd better take this down to the police station,' and she said, 'Yes,' her face suddenly grave.

She came back to the workshop half an hour later, with a thin man in plain clothes who she introduced as Sergeant Crittenden.

'A fine can of worms you've opened here, Mr

Morgan!' I don't know why he blamed *me* for opening it; but antique dealers get blamed for most things. 'We've sent on the gun to Forensic, and if it tallies with anything criminal, the shirt might give us a lead – there's a laundry mark on it. You were, of course, quite right to fetch it in. But the problem doesn't end there. The question is, what else might you turn up?'

'God knows,' I said. 'Anything.'

'The secrets of all hearts shall be revealed,' said James sententiously. He's given to quoting scripture. Sergeant Crittenden gave him a pained look, and went on.

'*And* I've just chased four youngsters out of your drive. Not that they've run far – they're hanging around the gate now. It seems that these students' excitement is infectious – there are wild rumours of things buried in the Pond worth *thousands*.'

'Don't worry about me,' I said. 'I've got five-lever mortise locks, all my windows are nailed up, and I've got floodlights, alarms, closed-circuit TV . . .'

'It's not you I'm worried about. It's that Pond. A child has almost drowned there already. And if rumours of buried treasure get around . . .'

'Oh shit,' I said helplessly. 'Why couldn't the bloody students have kept their mouths shut . . .'

'You can't help human nature, Mr Morgan.' He said it rather helplessly too.

'We can pull out the ladders,' said Hermione tentatively, 'when we stop every evening. And chain them all together for the night.'

'They'll probably just bring their own.'

'If we had a couple of caravans,' Hermione added, 'some of the students could sleep on site and patrol. If we had permission . . .'

'I think that might be arranged,' said Sergeant Crittenden thoughtfully. 'And I know a man who runs second-hand caravan sales. He might help out. And you could do with some floodlights and a generator. And I could ask the beat-constables to give you regular back-up . . .'

They went wandering off together, Hermione planning and Sergeant Crittenden being helpful and protective . . . amazing girl, Hermione.

Another slime-covered object was carried in. A student washed it. A simple tin tugboat, about a foot long. No engine or anything. Little more than a pressed metal dish with a pointed bow, and a half-deck, and a hinged single funnel that folded down when not in use. Sixpence at Woolworth before the War. But the enamel paint on it was as bright as ever; painted-on doorways and handrails, and portholes with smiling childish faces peering out. Fetch well over a hundred quid, in that condition. Tin plate collectors are among the maddest collectors of all . . . a crying child loses it in 1936, and the next thing is, it's in the hands of some wealthy gloating adult. The world's a pretty mad place really.

Hell, here was something else, something big this time, that took two students to carry it. Even under the coating of slime I could tell what it was. That fat porpoise shape and the keel sticking out underneath. A professionally-built three-foot model sailing yacht. The kind grown-up blokes sailed in races, when they still wore boaters and blazers and white flannels to sail model yachts. James joined in the cleaning of it, his blunt fingers gentle, thoughtful, as he disentangled the rigging from the snapped-off mast. I could see I wasn't going to get much work out of him for the next few days . . .

CHAPTER FOUR

By tea-time, she had her caravans. And her generator and floodlights. That girl could twist men round her elegant little finger. Meanwhile, more stuff had been dug out – another priceless piece of German tin plate – an ocean liner this time, with four funnels. And a poor little wooden fishing-boat, with its side stove in by some bigger craft that had run it down, so many years ago. It was beyond repair; even James admitted that. And it was a home-made effort to begin with – the first item with no commercial value. Things in the workshop calmed down a bit. Especially as, up at the Pond, some of the bigger humps had only yielded the usual dumped prams and bicycles.

Still, I felt uncommonly weary, and was glad to lock up for the night. I brought the armoured cruiser and the liner to my living-quarters upstairs. Partly for security, and partly to gloat over. I wasn't going to have them long. As I cooked my evening meal, I kept picking them up and wondering what stories they could tell, if only they could speak. That's partly why I went into antiques in the first place – the romance of it. And though the first few times I was swindled knocked a lot of the gilt off the gingerbread, I'm still far from being purely commercial.

After my meal, I fell asleep in front of the telly. Not at all like me. I always associate falling asleep in a chair with being middle-aged, which I dislike intensely. So, half out of curiosity and half to punish myself for being a dozy old bugger, I got into my Volvo and drove up to the Pond. It was about ten; dusk was just falling, but they had their floodlights on already, with the generator running. The Pond, under a mixture of twilight and floodlight, had a faded, haunted look. And the four students were in a high state of excitement, prowling around with pickaxe handles in their hands. And the local beat-bobby was there, with a loud hailer.

'Expecting a lively night?' I asked.

'Little sods have been at it already. We've chased them off twice. They're still lurking in the bushes on the far side.'

One of the students, a red-haired lad called Rory, said, 'We're used to it. You always get trouble on a town dig. Even if there's nothing worth stealing. They come on site and do what damage they can. Kicking earth back into the trenches; pulling the polythene off. Just for the hell of it. We lost a lovely bit of wattle and daub at Colchester last summer. They took off the polythene, and then we had a cloudburst – washed the whole thing away. I could've killed them – brainless little sods. I don't know what the young are coming to, these days.'

I couldn't help grinning. Such indignation, and he couldn't have been more than nineteen himself.

'Here they come again.'

A chain of kids was forming, on the dried mud of the far shore. The loud hailer bellowed out.

'This is the police. Stay away from the Pond. One boy has already nearly drowned. The pond is *dangerous*. Stay away from the bank.'

With total indifference, the chain began to edge out into the mud.

'Oh shit,' said Rory. 'Here we go again.' The students began to run around the shore, two one way and two the other. They ran lethargically, without hope. It was a long way round. But the chain of kids seemed to think they had found something. The one at the end, up to his ankles in mud, was digging with his hands frantically, while the next in line held on to the belt of his jeans.

They left it too long, in their eagerness. The running pairs of students suddenly sensed success, and increased their speed. The kids saw their danger; the ones nearest the shore broke away and headed into the bushes. The next three began casting anxious glances, and shouting warnings to each other, which came across the Pond as faint as bird-calls. Then the three of them broke and ran, leaving just the kid on the end, who had hauled something out of the mud and stood straddle-legged with it in his arms.

He too made a bolt for the shore. But the mud on his boots impeded him; and the weight in his arms. The students closed in, he tried to swerve past them, there was the flash of a pickaxe handle, and a yelp of pain. Then they were manhandling him back around the Pond towards us, one of them carrying the muddy treasure.

The kid was about fourteen. He was smothered in mud from head to foot, and limping badly, where the pickaxe handle had done its work.

'Ain't done nuffin',' he shouted at the policeman. 'It's a public park. An' what I got is anybody's property! What gives this lot the right to it? Some kid lost it. Finders keepers.'

'There is a crime called stealing-by-finding,' said the bobby, with what conviction he could muster. 'Anything you find should be taken to a police station, as lost property.'

'Are this lot doing that, then?' The boy glared round at the students. 'The police station must be getting a bit muddy! I *heard* it was all going down to old Jeff Morgan's shop!'

'Everything they find is reported to us,' said the copper, without conviction.

'An' what about the crime of criminal assault?' shouted the kid. 'He hit me wi' that pickaxe handle. I'm sure he's broke something. I'll get my mum to get a lawyer on *you*!'

'Push off,' said the bobby. 'Before I run you in.' The kid took a hard look at Rory, as if memorizing his face for some future identity parade. Then he slouched off, turning at twenty yards distance to shout again about criminal assault. It was a long time before he finally went away.

'He's right, you know,' said the bobby, turning to Rory. 'It was you I should have charged. Assault. Carrying an offensive weapon. You shouldn't have done that!'

'Well, what are we supposed to do?' yelled Rory. 'If it goes on this way, they could ruin the dig.'

'Kids know more about the bloody law than we do, these days. I'm afraid they've got us by the short and curlies. I'm *really* here to make sure they don't drown themselves . . .'

There was a depressed silence. Then I said, 'What had he got? Anything valuable?'

The object was held up. 'A Star yacht,' said Rory.

'They're ten a penny. They're still making them. You can buy them in the shops. Ten quid.' Then he added, 'It could have been something priceless.'

'Look,' said somebody. 'There they go again.' Another line of kids was venturing out on to the mud, on the far side.

It was indeed a lively evening. By half-past ten, the constable was hoarse with yelling through the loud hailer, and the rest of us were exhausted with running. By and large, the luck had been with us; we'd stopped the kids getting away with anything. But a very nice carvel-built yacht had been trodden on, in the fray, and crushed like an eggshell.

'Hundreds of hours' work!' said Rory bitterly, surveying the wreck.

'I'll see what my bloke can do with it,' I said, to comfort him. 'It's only down one side. It'll do for a museum, if you turn that side to the wall . . .'

Suddenly, there was a hiss in the air above my head, and something pinged on the caravan's side. We stared at a neat round black hole, a quarter of an inch wide.

'There's a kid out there with a bloody airgun!' said the bobby, glaring at the nearest rhododendrons. He took off towards the place it had come from, like an Olympic athlete.

But he came back, sweating and empty-handed. 'I heard him crashing through the bushes. But it's like a jungle in there.'

There was another hiss and ping; this time from the direction of the generator.

'He's trying to put out the floodlights!' shouted Rory.

Then a large piece of brick came hurtling through the air. Followed by several more.

'That's *it*!' roared the constable, at the end of his tether. He spoke into his radio and summoned back-up.

I must say, the police put up a splendid show. Two pandas arrived, blue lights flashing. They slammed in through the Park gates, and roared all the way round the path that followed the shore of the Pond. It was most impressive.

'That should settle the little sods,' said the constable, when they'd gone again. 'It's gone eleven. I suppose they've got *some* homes to go to.'

He must have been right. Nothing stirred round the shores of the Wheatstone Pond.

'Been like a bloody madhouse,' he added, picking up his loud hailer. 'I don't know what's got into the kids round here. This is normally a quiet district. For London.'

It was then that, back at the shop, my burglar-alarm went off. I would recognize that dreadful whooping anywhere. I was into my car and belting down Wheatstone High Street before I knew what I was doing.

And, in my headlights, I saw them running out of my gate. Two slim figures in trainers, jeans and bomber jackets. They turned for a second to stare at me, shielding their eyes against my lights.

And for some reason I went berserk. I mean, I've always hated burglars, especially with regard to my shop, because it's my living. If they burgle the house, well, it's just kids after videos to sell for drugs, and you can replace a video with the insurance money. But if they go for the shop, they're pros, and they're after the things you've sweated over . . .

But that night ... they were running along the pavement now, pinned by the lights against the high walls ...

I had a sudden mad desire to flatten them against that wall; to never have to worry about them again. They were ... no more than insects ...

It was lucky for them they had a car waiting with the rear doors open. They vanished inside; the car revved up, smoke spouting from its exhaust ...

I aimed straight for it. And almost forgot to slam on the brakes.

I can't have been doing more than fifteen, when I hit it. I felt the seat-belt tighten across my chest. Then the massive front of the Volvo was driving the rear end of their car along the bricks of the wall in a brilliant shower of sparks. Crushing it up like an egg. I could see it was a Citroën AX they'd got; by comparison with the Volvo they're not very heavily built.

A sudden silence. Then I was out of the car. Somebody tried to get out of the front door of the AX. I slammed the car door on his extended leg, and heard with joy a squeal of pain.

Then a policeman from the Pond had hold of me, was shouting at me, shaking me. And slowly I came back to my senses.

It was two in the morning before it was all sorted out, and then the duty inspector took me into his office. He was much younger than I was; in fact he didn't look more than a sixth former, with his chubby rosy cheeks. But his face was solemn. *Very* solemn.

'All's well that end's well, Mr Morgan.' His tone quite belied his words. 'Nobody hurt, beyond cuts and bruises. By a *miracle*. And we mustn't expect too many *miracles*, must we, Mr Morgan?'

He was talking to me as if I was a kid.

'I'm entitled to make a citizen's arrest,' I said, nastily.

'It's only a *miracle* it wasn't a citizen's multiple murder. It's lucky you're not in the cells now. What the hell did you think you were doing?'

'I suppose I misjudged the distance. But they were getting away. Like they so often do with burglaries. Even with our magnificent police force . . .'

He just stared at me. Then he said, 'Are you a *violent* man, Mr Morgan? All we have on our records about you is one case of drunk and disorderly.'

'That was the week after my wife died.' That made him flinch a little. But he didn't like me any more for it.

'You had no evidence they were even burglars . . . then.'

'Running out of my gate at gone eleven, with the burglar-alarm going? I hardly imagined they were Jehovah's Witnesses.'

'They could have been passers-by, trying to help.'

'Why did they go running, then?'

'Perhaps they panicked and thought you were going to knock them down. They *say* they were very frightened. They *say* they thought their last hour had come . . .'

'But they *were* burglars.' I wasn't letting him get away with anything. The nerve, looking me up in criminal records . . . as if I was a common felon.

'Yes, luckily for you, we found tools on them that constitute an offence in themselves. Which gave us grounds to search their homes. We found enough. They won't bother us now for a bit . . . but *you* bother me a lot, Mr Morgan . . .'

'We'd had a lot of hassle up by the Pond . . .'

'So I hear. University undergraduates hitting people with pickaxe handles. There seems to be something about that Pond, Mr Morgan, that comes between law-abiding citizens and their wits. I shall be profoundly glad when it's filled in and being used as tennis-courts . . . well, that will be all, for now. I only hope you realize what a very narrow escape you've had.' He didn't shake hands; he pointedly lowered his head to begin reading a pile of report-forms, and left me to find my own way out.

I got home. Some workman recommended by the police had made my shop door secure with a huge piece of thick plywood. I went upstairs and poured myself a stiff drink, and stared at the little armoured cruiser and the smaller ocean liner, side by side, glinting in the lamplight.

And finally I admitted that something had got into me tonight. Something I'd hardly known before. Something I didn't like at all. Something I hadn't felt since I was twelve, in a fight in the school yard. I had wanted, for a little while, to kill.

The thought somehow congealed with an older thought. My feelings of guilt about the silly young fool who had killed himself on the motorbike I'd sold him. Why had death suddenly come into my life, after all these years? All these hardworking peaceful years? Was there *really* something odd about the Wheatstone Pond?

41

It was then I noticed the light on my telephone-answering machine was glowing, and pressed the play-back.

It was Hermione. Triumphant.

'Best bib and tucker tomorrow morning, Jeff. We've got a television crew coming. Ten sharp, or so they say. I'll be round by half-past eight. There'll be a lot to work out.'

I stared at the machine as if it was the author of all my misfortunes. How on earth had she got the telly people in so quickly? There'd been no mention of them when we parted. I supposed she had contacts, being press officer for the City Toy Museum . . .

But was she *mad*? The last thing we needed was publicity. We'd have the kids from half of London after us tomorrow night . . .

With a groan, and a curse, I flung myself into bed, to get what sleep I could. Damned conniving woman . . .

CHAPTER FIVE

We were all gathered in my lounge for the end of the six o'clock news. Watching the weather forecast quack on, and waiting for the local slot. They'd left their wellies by the door, but my carpet was still getting pretty muddy.

We were the first item; it was beginning to be the silly season, and they must be short of hard stuff. We were introduced by our very own girl-reporter, Bunny Hodkinson, small and blonde and cuddly, with huge innocent blue eyes and the naïve grin of a pretty rabbit. Just the sort any male would open his heart to. I mean, whoever heard of a man-eating rabbit?

There she was, standing on the bank, peering out over the mud. Then she turned to the camera confidingly and said, 'The Wheatstone Pond is beautiful in summer; but the Wheatstone Pond can be a killer. There have been seven suicides on this spot in the last five years. Now Wheatstone Council have decided its days are numbered. Once it is pumped dry, it will be filled in, and made into tennis-courts.

'The Pond is being pumped dry by appliances from the London Fire Brigade . . .'

So then we had the station officer, wearing full fire-fighting gear and his lovely big helmet, for no reason any of us could guess at. But he made a big thing of the danger of the mud and slime and the way kids were risking their lives. Ending up, 'Not a nice death, with your mouth full of mud and your lungs full of green slime.'

One up to Hermione; it would have frightened *me* off; but would it frighten the kids? Or would it be an excuse for them to play chicken?

We had a few seconds of a girl student with a curvy bottom, crawling along one of the ladders. Then the camera panned on to what we were starting to call the dump. All the useless prams and bikes and children's tricycles we'd unearthed, that no thief would want to nick. It looked spectacularly horrible, trailing strands of dried grey slime. Then it panned across to Hermione, who was wearing what any chic archaeologist would be wearing, providing she didn't have to get her hands dirty.

'It's heart-breaking work,' she said, with a carefully rueful smile. 'Nine out of ten of the things we find are just rubbish that people have dumped.'

Two up to Hermione. Who wants to risk their neck for a pram with four bent wheels?

'But what exactly are you hoping to find?' Bunny fed Hermione the agreed question. At this point the filming stopped and we moved to my workshop. Which had, of course, been cleared of everything of value, apart from a wardrobe that James was repolishing.

And here was James himself, with the camera panning on to him. He was holding what appeared to be a three-foot-long shallow, narrow dish made up of charred wood. With a tall cylinder sticking up from the middle of it, surrounded by blackened cylindrical objects and wheels.

'What exactly *is* it?' Disbelief and distaste mingled

in our own girl-reporter's voice. James opened his own mouth, preparing an oration ... oh, foolish James! Hermione had nipped in front of him, before he could draw breath.

'This is rather pathetic really. It's a Victorian model steamboat – I mean, actually powered by a steam-boiler, with a methylated-spirit stove underneath to heat the water. Unfortunately, in this case, the spirit-stove must have overturned or leaked, setting the wooden super-structure on fire. It burnt the hull right down to the water-line, sadly, before the little ship finally sank. It must have been heart-breaking for the proud child who owned it . . .'

'But quite a spectacular sight for any bystanders,' said Bunny callously. 'Steaming round, going up in flames. Then sinking. Like the *Titanic* in miniature, really.' She sounded like she would have liked to have been there with her camera crew. At the real *Titanic* disaster too. Everything brought grist to her mill . . .

'What can you do with it now?'

Poor old James opened his mouth again, but once more Hermione nipped in. James was being reduced to a hard-breathing display-stand.

'Oh, we can dry out what's left of the woodwork and preserve it. And remove the mechanical parts and polish them up. If we can find a maker's name-plate, we could possibly look up the model in an old maker's catalogue, and build a replica – wreck and replica displayed side by side. Or at least the photograph from the catalogue, greatly enlarged.'

'Oh yes, fascinating,' said our girl-reporter, without a lot of conviction in her voice. 'But this . . . wouldn't be worth anything? In the open market?'

'Definitely not,' said Hermione, with a sudden tightening of her jaws. 'Only of interest to our City Toy Museum.'

'But we've heard you've found things of real value, Mr Morgan ... you're taking part in this ... dig ... but you're also an antique dealer with a knowledge of prices. Has anything of value been found?'

I was ready, with breath already in my lungs; so I got in while Hermione was still opening her pretty mouth. And I had a carefully-selected table of items beside me. The first was the cheap tin tugboat from Woolworth.

'*That* looks exciting,' said Bunny dubiously. 'What's that worth?'

'Well, to a *fanatical* collector of tin-plate toys, about a hundred pounds. At a specialist auction – Sotheby's or something. But it's not the kind of thing anybody could hope to flog round the nearest pub. I mean, how much would you give for it, in a pub?'

'Couple of quid?' asked Bunny, wrinkling up her pretty little nose.

'Exactly,' I said. 'Tin-plate-toy collectors are the maddest folk in the business. And that thing cost sixpence in Woolworth, before the War.'

I went on holding up dreary items for the camera. The crushed yacht, the little fractured fishing-boat, the Star yacht that anybody could buy for ten quid.

The camera watched Bunny's face fall. 'So you haven't had much luck, so far?'

'We found a loaded revolver. But we passed that straight across to the police. It had been fired twice ... it could be a murder weapon.'

Oh, how her little face lit up! The camera cut to the

local nick, where Sergeant Crittenden said the police were waiting for a lab report.

I really thought we'd got away with it. I drew a deep breath of relief.

But then we were back in my workshop again. And she was opening her sweet girlish lips for the fatal question.

'But I believe you did find *one* item of value – a motorbike – an antique motorbike? Which you sold for a good price – to a young man who later killed himself on it?'

The camera panned on to my face. My mouth, wide open as I absorbed the body-blow. I looked a guilty crook found out, even to myself. A guy who sold dodgy motorbikes, on which people killed themselves. I watched myself trying to say something three times. I watched myself break out into a sweat. Just like those guys who *That's Life* pillory on their own door-steps.

The camera cut, before I said, 'It had an MOT test and passed it successfully.' On to the next item – a fuss about a welfare centre for ethnic lesbians, in the Red Republic of Brent. Somebody had the grace to switch the bloody set off.

'The bitch,' I said. 'The little bitch!'

There was a rumbled murmur of agreement, from the assembled workers. But Hermione just said cheerfully, 'Don't worry, Morgan, it'll be a nine day's wonder. You aren't going to be selling any more motorbikes anyway. The main thing is, I think that'll have killed off the enthusiasm of our treasure-hunters.'

'I hope so,' said Rory, in a very heartfelt tone.

'Unless they start thinking the lake is full of revolvers . . . Well, back to guard-duty . . .'

But I think they had a pretty quiet night.

It was nearly lunch-time, the next day, when Lenny turned up with the box. A strong wooden box, about two feet long and nine inches wide, and dark with still-dripping water. We'd had a steady stream of objects all morning; the best of which was a long narrow object that turned miraculously into a slim white speed-boat, with a covered-in bow and a long brass boiler, and a propeller stuck out behind on a long shaft.

'Heck,' I said. 'A Meccano Hornby steam-launch. I'd forgotten that they *existed*. Not many people had them. I wanted one, but I could never save up enough. They cost a bomb, even in 1939 . . .'

'Well, you can't afford one now, either,' said dear Hermione. 'Hands off, Morgan. Down, dog.'

I gave her a look. And it was at that point that Lenny walked in with the box. I was getting a bit fed up with Lenny. He was my youngest worker; my errand-boy really. And his legitimate errands were taking longer and longer. I mean, I had sent him off to deliver a couple of leather chairs to Hampstead two hours ago. And even allowing for traffic . . . now I had proof he'd been wasting time hanging round the Pond. The Pond was rapidly coming between him and his senses. I was going to have a word with him. But it would have been quite useless at the moment. He could think about nothing but the box.

'*I'm* going to open it. *I'm* going to open it. It's *my* turn.'

Pathetic.

I looked at that box, while he was rummaging for a screwdriver among the benches. Somehow, I didn't like the look of that box. It was well made, of thick plywood that had survived its soaking, and it was screwed down tight, with no less than eight screws. And from the way he'd been carrying it, and put it down, it was heavy.

Somebody had not wanted that box to be found. Or opened. Too many screws; screws beyond sense. I began to edge away from the crowd that was gathering round Lenny; edge towards the door. Almost as if it might be a bomb. Though the idea of a bomb going off after all that soaking was pretty unlikely. But my silly body insisted on edging away. Even before I smelt the smell. Now I admit that my workshop has never smelt like a bed of roses. Too much boiling of glue; the odd pot of rancid size; welding . . . and it hadn't smelt any sweeter since they began carrying in things covered with stinking ooze. But *this* smell . . .

From the doorway, I paused and looked at them. All the avid faces, like something out of a painting by Bruegel, or a medieval Doom. Hermione, James, Rory, the tall bland Dane they called Sven.

'Two more screws,' called out Lenny hysterically. 'It's coming, it's coming.'

Now Hermione had noticed the smell; her nostrils were twitching. And James was backing up and flinching; it was a smell he must have smelt often in Italy. Even bland Sven was looking worried. But Lenny, impervious to everything but excitement, was undoing the last screw. He prised up the lid.

I think he tried to say something; but his breath was overtaken by the vomit rising in his throat. He made a feeble lunge for the nearest Belfast sink, but he didn't make it. He spewed up uncontrollably all over the shavings on the floor; all down his own front. James swung away, grabbing a grubby handkerchief from his apron pocket and pressing it to a face turned green. Sven just stood, paralysed, giant hands clenched so tight the knuckles showed white. Only Hermione kept her cool, though she was ghost-pale. She stepped to one side, and I saw it, at the distance of ten yards. I never wanted to get any nearer.

A tiny skull, tilted, peered out of the box. Below it, there might have been fabric; but it was mottled with patterns of green and brown, like damp patches on a ceiling; like mould on cheese.

They all came bundling towards the door where I stood, like a routed army, stumbling, groping. I got aside quickly, to let them past. Rory was half-carrying Lenny, who was making a weird keening noise in his throat.

Hermione came out last. She said, faintly, 'You'd better ring the police.'

For some reason I said stupidly, 'An abortion?' Perhaps I thought that if it was an abortion it wouldn't be quite so bad.

'No.' Her words came out slowly, one by one, as if she was inventing them. 'Somebody . . . cared. It's . . . wrapped . . . in some kind of shawl. There's a little crucifix on its . . . chest.'

I got them all into my kitchen, and put a kettle on before I rang the police.

'Whisky, Morgan, for Christ's sake. Bloody *tea* won't do any good.' It was not really her voice. 'I'll stand on guard at the shed door. Before anybody else blunders in and sees it.'

I must say the police were quick. Two uniformed constables leaping out of the panda. Perhaps they were not well informed; they came out of my workshop a damned sight quicker than they went in. I offered them a tot of whisky as well, and for once they didn't refuse. One said weakly, 'Jeez, I thought I'd seen everything in this game, but . . .'

None of us seemed able to move from the kitchen, till they came and took it away.

After supper, I felt a bit better; I took a stroll up to the Pond. I don't know what drew me. There was nothing to see; no kids, no students on guard. Nobody at all, really, except one elderly man walking his elderly fox-terrier, and bullying it into hurrying up to do its business. It was a grey cloudy dusk; it was as if a pall lay over the whole Pond; as if that smell, from my workshop, had driven everyone out of Wheatstone, like an outbreak of plague.

CHAPTER SIX

We held a meeting, the next morning, in the workshop. Hermione said we'd better hold it there; get them in there again quickly, before they got spooked with the place. There were fifteen of us, I recall. Ten students, Hermione, James, Sam my other furniture restorer, me and Sergeant Crittenden. Of Lenny, there was no sign. And the rest of us looked weary and wretched. I kept on sniffing, surreptitiously, to see if I could still smell that smell. So did everybody else.

I must say, Crittenden was very good. He sort of got us on a war-footing. I didn't reckon he'd ever rise higher than sergeant, but he was a good sergeant. Immaculately turned out; none of this tie-halfway-down-his-chest, like most of the CID. His dark hair Brylcreemed like a shining black cap. He was not so young as I'd thought at first; quite wrinkled in his pale way, but oddly handsome in a stark fashion.

'First a bit of good news,' he said. 'That revolver you found – it has been of some help to us. It *was* used in a murder – of an old occult book-dealer called Solomon Hertz. Down the Charing Cross Road. The bullets match two taken from the body. So that's cleared up. The murder was never solved . . .'

Suddenly everyone was intensely interested. Everyone likes to be part of a hunt.

Then he gave a wry smile. 'But since the murder took place in 1921 – before most of your parents were born – it doesn't get us much further. However, you will be relieved to know that since sixty-six years have passed, we think it unlikely the murderer will strike again . . .'

It was just the right touch; wry, bitter, Met black humour. It stiffened us; gave us a little of their professionalism.

'I've had a little talk about you with my boss. He sends his sympathetic regards. And a few bits of advice.' He counted them off on his stubby fingers.

'One. Anything ambiguous – anything that you can't make out what it is – call us in straight away. *Don't* think you're being a nuisance – we'd rather be safe than sorry. You were a bit silly yesterday – that box could've contained anything. Even Semtex explosive. The IRA are not above dumping stuff quickly if they get into a jam. And even if it's been under water, a bomb can still go off under certain circumstances . . . I'm only glad we're not here this morning picking little bits of you off the telephone-wires . . .'

That got the start of a snort of grim laughter. It *is* quite nice to think you might have been blown to bits, and instead still have two arms and two legs. It makes you feel ahead of the game.

'Two. You can expect to find almost anything. That Pond is a dumping ground for guilty secrets – half of London's guilty secrets, for all we know. It wouldn't surprise me if you found more infant bodies – there were a lot dumped in the old days, when we didn't have these NHS abortion clinics, and it still happens sometimes, even now. Use your noses, and you'll save yourselves a lot of grief.'

There it was. Out in the open. Talked about in a matter-of-fact way. A normal, if grim, part of life. Something the Met had to handle every day, and if *they* could handle it, so could we . . .

'On the other hand, I'm expecting you to find some rifles too. Not an IRA cache.' (He actually smiled.) 'No, a lot of poor buggers in the First World War, who were home on leave, and didn't want to go back to the front, got into the habit of dumping their gear in the nearest standing water. Their kitbags usually floated, but the rifles went straight to the bottom. We sometimes get them turned in by people doing your kind of job when the Thames is at low water . . . mudlarks, we call them.'

Again a grim rumble of humour from the group. And also a prick of interest.

'If you find a rifle, for God's sake don't fiddle with the trigger – a round up the spout can still go off after seventy years, and if the barrel's blocked with mud, it turns into a bomb that can make quite a mess.'

They were really laughing now.

'Likewise bombs and shells from the Second World War. I suppose you all know what a bomb looks like . . .? Got fins on the end of it.'

Having got them in a good mood, he finished by saying, 'You're doing a public service. This pond has got to be drained, and once it's drained, it's got to be searched. We don't want bombs or shells exploding under the new tennis-courts. And, frankly, the police have not got time to do the search themselves. You're freeing us for our proper job, which is catching criminals. Thank you. Any questions?'

Rory looked up and asked, 'How long before the Pond's fully dry, sergeant?'

'A long time yet. The fire brigade are on to a deeper bit at the south end. Even they don't know how deep *that* is. But that's quite useful, because the water from the rest of the mud is slowly draining into it. It should make your job a bit easier. Anything else?'

Everyone shook their heads sagely, and then they made a move for the door, sounding moderately cheerful. Only Hermione lingered behind.

'What about . . . that baby . . .?'

Crittenden stared at the floor. 'Murdered,' he said. 'The breastbone was smashed in – they think by a blow with a sharp implement.'

Hermione went as white as a sheet. 'When?'

'They think . . . within the last ten years. That's working from the type of plywood used to make the box. The strangest thing is . . . you know it was wrapped in something? Well, it was a piece torn from a linen bed-sheet. And there was a laundry-mark on that sheet and . . . it was the same laundry-mark as we found on that shirt wrapped around the revolver. Sixty years apart, and the same laundry-mark.'

'Have they traced the laundry?' I don't know how Hermione got the words out.

'They think it was a laundry that was bombed in the War, and never reopened. The trail's quite cold there, I'm afraid.'

'I never heard of anything so crazy . . .' I said.

He looked at me. 'No, it doesn't make sense, any kind of sense. Except that people keep sheets a very long time, locked up in linen-cupboards . . . I hear you people are still selling the public Victorian night-dresses at a good profit?'

'Not me,' I said. 'But some.'

'Stuff lasts a long time.' He flicked me an odd lopsided grin. 'But who am I to tell that to an antique dealer?' He turned to Hermione. 'What I have just told you is in confidence, madam. We want to keep quiet about this baby business at the moment, and I'm sure you don't want your work at the Pond held up by crowds of ghouls. In any case, I've asked the local panda to keep in close touch with you. Good day.'

And he went, leaving us staring at each other, speechless.

The next two days were fairly peaceful. The warm spell was developing into something of a heatwave, and the students, as brown as berries, worked in very short shorts and wellies. The huge saucer-shaped depression of the Pond now broke up into three areas. Close to shore, the drying mud was cracking into irregular plates a foot across, which the trampling feet crushed to a foul-smelling dust that hung in the hot air. Further out, the deep mud still glistened and popped, talking with a low chuckling noise that we no longer really heard. And at the south end, the fire appliance still pumped away at a figure-of-eight of black water.

The students could move on the dried-out part without ladders now, though some cracked patches were still treacherous, and one or two of them ended knee-deep in blackness. Sven even lost one of his wellies. A lot of smaller mounds were poking up, as drying-out continued, and there was a rush to investigate them before the thieving kids got to them. The kids were still lurking quite openly round the path, especially at lunch-time or after school, making occasional dashes to try to steal something. But Hermione had brought in ten more students, and they were strung out round the Pond fifty yards apart, and could usually head off any sudden invasion.

They found three rifles, just as Sergeant Crittenden had predicted, which made him some kind of god in their eyes. We took them straight to my shed and washed them off, and stacked them in one corner for the police to collect. Nobody tried to fire one, thank God. I handled the first one, a Lee Enfield .303, an ugly beast that no one would ever want to buy to hang on their wall. Then I lost interest. I'm not a weapons man, myself. James was inclined to muck about with them, wanting to clean and oil them, for old times' sake, and I had to speak sharply to him. We still had a living to make, and he had a job to do. It was odd, that. The way the stuff from the lake had a way of fascinating people, carrying them off into their dreams or their past. James talked a lot about his time in the Army in Italy.

Of Lenny there was still not a sign. Or word. I hoped he wasn't really ill. I felt I should go round to his house to find out; but what with the Pond and the shop, there was just too much to do. And I was *trying* to concentrate on the shop. I was dancing attendance on a well-dressed middle-aged woman who could not decide whether to buy a cast-iron doorstop in the form of a shepherd playing his pipe to his dog, or one in the shape of Punch, or both. I rather hoped she would buy Punch, for Punch was a good modern fake, but the shepherd was genuine, and I was rather fond of him.

At this point Sven burst in.

'Hermione want you! Now!'

I'm afraid I snarled at him; we'd all gone a bit jumpy since we found the plywood box, and the heat in my shop didn't help.

'Can't it wait? I was up there only an hour ago.'

'Is good news, I think.'

'Right, Sven. Will you wait here, until this lady has made her *mind* up, and take her cheque and write the number of her cheque card on the back of it and bring the cheque up to me. And lock the shop door behind you, and put the sign to "Back in fifteen minutes". Think you can remember all that?'

My outburst should have driven the poor little woman clean out of my shop empty-handed. But instead it flustered her into saying she would take both doorstops. The public's funny that way. She was so flustered she didn't even ask if she could have something off the price, which most of them never forget to do. So I drove up to the Pond in a mood of grim satisfaction.

Hermione met me, smiling. I could almost have imagined she was fond of me, and not just using me for her own ends.

'It's your big lucky day, Jeff!'

'The Crown Jewels have turned up, then? Wrapped up in a Buck House laundry-bag?'

Her mysterious smile widened, maddeningly. 'Noooooh. But you remember that story you told me – about one Guy Fawkes' Night and a man with a big model destroyer that sank? I think we've found it for you.' She led the way to the dump, and pulled a lump of sacking off something. Even under all the mud, I was pretty sure she was right. Two funnels, and the

58

mast blown off and trailing beside it, on the end of the tangle of rigging.

'And it's all yours,' she said.

I gaped at her.

'Well, we can hardly classify it as a children's toy, can we? We have to draw the line somewhere. It's an adult's hand-built scale model. Quite outside our remit. The museum wouldn't give it house-room. Though if you restored it nicely, it would look quite well in our preliminary exhibition . . .'

I knew there had to be a snag somewhere. That model would cost a bit to restore to glory . . . But I wasn't looking a gift-horse in the mouth.

Of course, once I got it back to the workshop, I couldn't resist fiddling with it. While my shop remained closed-for-fifteen-minutes, James gave me resentful looks because I was playing with my boat when I hadn't let him play with his rifle. He twice tried to interrupt me about some bloody woman and a set of stair-rods I'd promised her. But I just gave him the shop keys and got on with the boat.

The name on the bow was *Viperous*. One of the old 'V' class. *Vindictive* and all that lot. And the damage the fireworks had wreaked was fairly frightful. Not only was the mast blown off, but the metal plates of the hull had sprung apart in three places, which is why she'd sunk. The radio-control and even the electric motor were write-offs, and the damage the acid leaking from the batteries had done . . . it would take a real pro to restore her; even James couldn't cope. She was going to cost me a thousand quid. Dear old Hermione!

On the other hand, the detailing was so perfect . . .

even little brass breech-blocks on the guns in the open turrets . . . it would be worth it. I'd have a ship worth two thousand at least. I began wondering who I could get to do it . . .

And then I thought: suppose I did get it repaired? And put it up for auction? What about providing a provenance? And it really belonged to that ginger-haired idiot who'd sailed her on Guy Fawkes' Night, so long ago. He'd only been a young bloke . . . almost certain he was still alive . . . and still interested in model boats. Suppose he turned up and claimed her? I'd get a name as a real crook, and lose a thousand quid into the bargain. Probably end up in the magistrates' court . . . that would help my business, I must say. I paced up and down in a rare taking, stopping every two minutes to look at the boat again. I spent a very ratty afternoon, before I had an idea. I would consult Mossy Hughes. He was usually in the Duke of Portland in the early evening. Come to that, he was in the Duke of Portland most of the time. I put on my linen jacket and went for a pint.

The Duke of Portland is the nearest thing Wheatstone has to a local. A huge, florid building in moulded and glazed brown brick, a mass of ill-executed classical detail, pediments, pilasters and cartouches. A hideosity that would last for ever, or a bloody good architectural joke, depending how you were feeling. The frosted-glass windows and the mahogany in the public bar are genuine, though.

Mossy was in the public bar, leaning on the counter in the usual place, where his elbow has worn a hole in the shiny varnish. Mossy was a mystery to us all. He certainly never did a day's work. No visible means of support. If you asked he just said he was 'retired', though I suppose he couldn't be much over fifty. And he would never say what he had retired *from*. But, for a retired bloke, he had an amazing amount to spend buying drinks for other people. He saw me the moment I walked through the door, leapt athletically through the early evening crowd in his jeans and trainers, clasped me firmly by the elbow and said, 'What're you drinking, Mr Morgan?'

'Half of Guinness Bitter, Mossy, thanks!'

'A pint, a pint. What good's a half to a working man?' I watched him go, little athletic figure, fit as a flea. Some people thought he had private means. Personally, I thought he was a burglar. Working nights. A quiet, discreet and caring burglar, who spent his day doing good, lending a sympathetic ear to all and sundry, even lending hard-up acquaintances the odd fiver here and there, though he never lent a second note unless the first had been repaid.

Now he came back with two brimming pints, put them precisely into the centres of a pair of beer-mats, sat down, and cocked his head of grey hair, stiff and upright as a hairbrush, in a manner indicating he had all the time in the world to listen to my problems. It was as if he had no problems of his own, and felt the lack.

'What's bothering you, squire?'

'One Guy Fawkes' Night, about 1980 it would be. Crowd round the Pond watching the fireworks over the Heath.'

'I go every year, every year. Won't be the same without the Pond, will it? Though that *smell* . . .'

'Bloke . . . a nutter . . . tried to sail a model boat.

They blew it to bits with fireworks. You don't know who he was, do you?'

He put a hand to his brow, which had resolved into the most perfect set of horizontal wrinkles I had ever seen on any man. I counted them again. There were seven, one above the other. I could have sworn there'd been only six, the last time I counted. Mossy was still developing, evolving . . .

Finally, Mossy said, 'Tanner, his name was. Tony Tanner. Had had a lot of trouble with his missis, and walked out in the end. He was living in a bed-sitter, when I last talked to him. Up Belvoir Road. But that must have been six, seven year ago. Never seen him since. Must have gone off soon after that Guy Fawkes' Night. He was in a bad way, Mr Morgan. Drinking hard. Drinking to knock himself silly. Every night. Then he suddenly wasn't here any more. You know what bed-sitter land's like. What you want him for?'

'The boat that sank's turned up. Bit of a wreck. I wanted to make him an offer for it.'

'He told me he had a few boats, up in his room in Belvoir Road. Invited me up to see them, once, but I didn't get round to it.'

That figured. Mossy operated his alcoholic Samaritan service in the public bar of the Duke of Portland and nowhere else. Wise man. Safety in numbers.

'You don't know what number Belvoir Road?'

'House called Abbey-something. Abbeygate, Abbey-field? Third or fourth along on the right hand side, Tanner said. Said it had domes with spikes on top; like a German helmet. Said it gave him the bloody willies, but it was cheap.'

*

62

I got away from Mossy in the end. After another couple of pints. I reckoned I'd better walk the drink off, so I might as well walk up to Belvoir Road and try to find Abbey-something. Belvoir Road's not far; the first road above the Pond; the back gardens run down the hill to the edge of the Park.

I must say, Abbeywalk, when I found it, gave *me* the willies too. It made the other Gothic fantasies in the road look quite homely. Because it wasn't really Gothic in style; more a sort of sickly art nouveau. The window-frames looked like they'd begun to melt and droop in folds. There was a large and weird glass canopy over the front door. I just walked up to it. There was no front gate, and the weeds in the thin gravel drive were two feet high and dead. Last summer's. Or the summer before that. Not a sign of a car, or any other sign of life. The ground-floor windows were opaque with sawdust and cobwebs. A large plywood sign, starting to peel back into its separate layers, announced that the ground floor had once housed Abbeywalk Fine Fitted Kitchens, but the sawdust was grey and old, and there was no sound of industry within.

There was, however, a row of faded red plastic buttons on a black-speckled brass box screwed to the door-jamb. With names behind strips of plastic. Sometimes crossed out, with another name squeezed in above; all faded to a greater or lesser degree. And one of the most faded crossed-out ones was A. Tanner; neatly typed, but a ghost on the verge of extinction.

Tanner had been there; Tanner was gone. For some reason, it angered me greatly, that he should have escaped me. Now the wrecked destroyer would hang around my workshop gathering dust for ever, and with me not daring to do a damned thing about it.

So, reluctant to quite let go, I walked round the back of the house. The back door was as solidly bolted and unmoving as the front. All the windows had that coating of sawdust. But there was a little brick building, about the size of a garage, and the green blistering door of that was slightly ajar. I went over and pushed at it. It gave, but only a little. I pushed harder; very hard indeed in my anger. There was the sound of something like cardboard splitting, and now the door gave way enough for me to poke my head through, into the dim glimmer that came from yet another dusty window.

The place, once whitewashed, was piled high with suitcases. Old, bulging suitcases, with straps round them. Cardboard boxes, full of what looked like jumble; a battered electric kettle, two dusty floral cushions, a scarf trailing down the outside of a box. One box had burst open, spilling out woolly bobble-hats and gloves.

And among all this worthless tat lay askew a lovely scale model of a paddle-steamer; the sort that used to ply round the Kent coast to Margate and Ramsgate. It had been roughly tossed in upside-down, and the foremast was broken off short, sticking out at me like an accusing finger. The name on the bow was *Royal Daffodil*.

It could only have belonged to the man who made the wrecked destroyer . . . and then I realized what the jumble really was. The detritus of bed-sitters. Stuff left behind and never sent for. Chucked out here by a landlord whose patience was obviously exhausted, if its battered and knocked-about appearance was anything to go by.

I wanted to plunge in and rescue the *Royal Daffodil* there and then. But it was impossible. The bursting of boxes that had let me push my head round the door had released an avalanche of stale, damp-smelling worldly goods that ensured the door would open not another quarter of an inch. And I certainly wasn't going in for burglary in broad daylight, or carrying a three-foot paddle-steamer home under my arm.

So, with reluctance, I let the door swing to, and managed at least to get the sneck on, so it was not obviously ajar.

I walked back, wildly lusting after the *Royal Daffodil* and wondering, just a little, what had happened to its late owner.

As I passed the public bar entrance to the Duke of Portland I hesitated, hovered. A feeling was coming over me that I knew all too well. A temptation to do something dodgy. I fought against it for a minute, but I knew I was going to give in. The paddle-steamer had been slowly growing bigger and bigger in my mind. Lying there unloved, defenceless in that old outhouse.

You might think that thieves do a lot of harm in the world of antiques; but they don't really. I mean, they don't harm the antiques. I mean, what's the point of stealing something if you're not going to look after it? Every bit of damage drops the price ... no, the people who do harm to antiques are the nutters and vandals who smash them up. I mean, somebody may nick a Van Gogh from the Tate and it may vanish for years, but you know it's safe somewhere, and will turn up none the worse eventually. Whereas those religious maniacs who attack works of art with razors, or acid, or shotguns, they're the ones who need putting away for life. And there are the less spectacular nutters who in the fifties smashed up long-case clocks for scrap, or the nutters in the sixties who painted good mahogany furniture canary-yellow and stuck floral transfers all over it. I remember one Viennese wall-clock that came into my shop. Somebody in the First World War had taken the eagle off the top and stamped it into dust in a burst of patriotic fervour. Then somebody else in the twenties had removed all the ornamental turned knobs, to make it look more 'modern'. Then somebody in the sixties had painted it bright blue, over mahogany veneer. And finally somebody in the eighties had thrown it into the dustbin, breaking the glass. Hounding a good clock to a slow death – worse than fox-hunting. The dustmen brought it to me, and after a fortnight's hard work, it was back perfect and worth five hundred, and it would go on living for ever. That's what I call a moral act . . .

Anyway, so I told myself, as I turned in at the door of the Duke of Portland. Mossy was still in his usual place.

'Any luck, squire?' Was the man clairvoyant?

'He's gone, all right. Everybody's gone, from the look of the place.'

'Dodgy old house, that!' I gave him an old-fashioned look. How did *he* know?

'So I've been told,' he said quickly. 'So I've been told.'

'I went round the back. There's another model boat in a sort of brick outhouse. On top of a lot of old junk. Thick with dust.'

'Shame,' he said, with a flick of interest. 'Shame how people neglect good stuff. Good as the destroyer, was it?'

'Maybe better.' I took a deep breath. 'I mean, if somebody brought it into my shop, I'd willingly pay him three Cs for it.'

'Good as that? Let me get you a pint, Mr Morgan.'

He came back with brimming glasses. It was fascinating how he placed them exactly in the centre of the beer-mats.

'Cheers.'

'What worries me,' I said, 'is if some vandals got to it. The door's jammed shut with the weight of stuff against it. But they might get in through the little window . . .'

'Quite,' he said. 'Quite.' And turned to the topic of the problems of Tottenham Hotspur Football Club.

About ten the next morning, a van pulled into my yard. A youth in spectacles mended with insulation tape came into my workshop.

'Got any interest in model boats?' he asked, shuffling diffidently.

'Depends,' I said, and walked out to the van with him.

The paddle-steamer was there, under a dirty white sheet of plastic. I checked it. It was in good nick, apart from the broken mast. Couple of lifeboats missing, but James could soon copy the ones that were left.

'Gorra couple more,' said the youth, and pulled off two more plastic sheets. A nice model of a tug in good nick. And a model of a North Sea lightship that had been dealt one savage blow that had flattened the superstructure half-way to the deck.

67

'How much you want for them?' James had come out for a nosy, so I had to keep up the charade.

'Three for the paddle-steamer and two and a half for the tug. Fifty for the lightship . . .'

'Throw in the lightship free and you've got a bargain.'

'Done.' Then he added, 'Mossy sent you a message. Dunno what it means, but he said to tell you that Tony Tanner left all his gear. Clothes, pots and pans, the lot. There were name-tags on the suitcases. That make sense?'

Half-way to my wad of notes, I paused. In one way, it made sense. In another, it made no sense at all.

Where the hell had Tony Tanner *gone*?

Come to that, where had all the other people gone, whose wretched possessions were piled in that little out-house?

'Bastards,' said James, which was very strong language for him. He was handling the wrecked lightship with grieving, loving hands.

'Reckon you can do anything with it?'

'Well, it's all there. Long job with a pair of pliers, that's all. Bit of soldering. 'Sa glass-case job, this. Never been in the water. Wouldn't float properly. No engine or anything. And there's a maker's name-plate. Ross and Makepeace. Number 18734.'

I pricked up my ears. I'd never heard that name before. But you live and learn, in our trade.

'Must look them up in a book,' I said.

'Probably worked for shipbuilders – *real* ship-builders I mean. You know, model to show the customer, afore the real one's built.'

'Yeah,' I said. And forgot about it. But not for long.

Then we had the business about the bomb; and then the business about the firemen.

The students were thrilled to bits to have found a bomb. Though it was only a very small one. They were thrilled to bits until the police arrived, and moved everyone away from the Pond, so that they couldn't get on with their work.

As we waited for the Bomb Disposal Squad, I was surprised at the amount they bickered among themselves. Really spiteful it was; they had one girl in tears. I truly felt like smashing a couple of the men's faces in for it. But Hermione went and smoothed things over, and brought the girl back to the caravan for a cup of tea. She was a pretty little thing called Ruth. A bit frail and forlorn; I suppose you could write her down as one of life's victims, but I liked her.

She sipped her tea and said, 'Bastards! This is the nastiest dig I've ever been on. People are so good-tempered, usually.'

'They *have* been a bit much,' said Hermione, running her hand through her hair. 'And it's getting worse. Sometimes I feel like sacking the lot of them, and getting in a fresh bunch.'

'Bloody good idea,' said Ruth feelingly. 'All girls for a change.'

'The girls are being as bad as the men,' said Hermione. 'Bitch, bitch, bitch.'

'Maybe it's the mud,' I said. 'And the smell. And those kids hanging around trying to nick stuff . . .'

'Rory really hurt one of them again this morning.

I'd not be surprised if the boy's mum came up. With a lawyer. Rory's not his usual cheerful self at all. I've worked with him before . . .'

It was just then we saw the firemen. Two of them, running along the edge of the Pond, one after the other, about twenty yards apart. They had stripped down to their vests in the heat, but were still in uniform on their lower parts.

The front one was carrying some sort of box, and throwing bits of white stuff from it into the Pond.

'What's this – a paper-chase?' asked Hermione, shading her eyes with her hand and staring at them. 'Now there's three of them.'

The third man, a hundred yards behind, was still in full uniform. He was running more reluctantly, somehow, and falling behind. And all three of them were shouting at each other.

They drew nearer.

'That's a sandwich-box,' said Hermione. 'He's throwing his sandwiches into the mud. Why? There's not a duck in sight.'

Now the leader was only fifty yards away; still turning his head to shout over his shoulder. He threw what looked like a small apple-pie into the Pond, and then what was certainly an orange.

And then, not looking where he was going, he tripped over the muddy frame of a bicycle, that somebody had dragged out of the Pond and left lying about; and went full-length. He was up in a flash, but limping now, and in another ten yards, the second man was on him.

I suppose we expected some kind of horseplay. It dawned on me that the first man must not have been throwing his own sandwiches into the Pond, but the sandwiches that belonged to the pursuing second man. Or perhaps we just expected a nasty argument. Certainly we never expected what happened.

A fist flew. There was a cry of pain, and the first man doubled up, holding his nose with fingers from which blood flowed.

The second fireman raised his boot and kicked him in the gut. He collapsed, screeching. Then the second man began to kick him as he lay writhing on the ground.

We all stood paralysed. I don't think we were cowards. We just couldn't believe our eyes. I mean, we're conditioned to think our London firemen are wonderful, even if we're starting to have doubts about our policemen. Firemen are supposed to rescue people: from burning buildings; from having their heads stuck through railings. Firemen are compassionate and caring: they come and rescue your dear pussy-cat, if it gets stuck up some tree.

Firemen do not kick each other to a bloody pulp.

It was lucky for the first man that the third man arrived when he did.

'Rogers!' he roared, with the voice of authority. 'Stop that!'

Rogers might have stopped for all of thirty seconds, then he aimed another kick at the groaning man.

'Rogers, I'm putting you on a charge!'

The kick went home, with a dull thud. The third man tried to grab the kicker. The kicker lashed out at him. He only just dodged back in time.

'Right, Rogers, you're suspended from duty, as of now.'

Rogers lashed out at his superior officer again, narrowly missing. The leading fireman backed off, and began to talk into his radio, which was clipped to his tunic. Now Rogers just stood, wild-eyed, panting. The man on the ground groaned horribly, and curled up into a tighter ball, hands holding his gut. I could tell he was really seriously hurt.

I felt I should go across and help him; but the wildness of the fist-clenched figure standing over him . . . it was Hermione who ran to help the injured man. Rogers nearly kicked her, till he saw she was a woman; he seemed as if he was coming out of some sort of fit. He seemed not to know where he was . . .

Now, in the distance, we could hear a siren. And at that dire sound, Rogers suddenly ran away round the edge of the Pond.

We all gathered round the man on the ground. But there wasn't much anyone could do. He yelled out in pain if you tried to touch him. He was violently sick, and I thought there were streaks of blood in the vomit.

A police car swung in through the Park gate. Two uniformed constables got out and stared at the groaning body.

'Who did it?'

The leading fireman pointed up the shore of the Pond, where Rogers was backing away further, and shouting something we couldn't make out. There was something so strange, so . . . crazy about the way he was pacing up and down and shouting incoherencies, that I saw the constables look at each other with raised eyebrows. Then one of them radioed for back-up, and they began to move up the shore fairly cautiously. I noticed that they stayed together.

Another siren. Two now. One would be an ambulance, I hoped. I didn't like the noises the man on the ground was making at all.

Ambulance and police car together. The ambulancemen very calm and slow-moving; the two fresh policemen making their way round the Pond the other way, talking into their radios.

We listened to them take the injured man away; but we watched Rogers across the water. There was something so strange and restless about him; more like some animal. He shouted at the policemen as they closed in; then there was a sudden rush of blue shirts, and he was face-down on the ground.

We turned away, letting out deep breaths of relief.

'What the hell was all that about?' I asked the leading fireman. He wiped a sweating face.

'Bloody sandwiches. They were larking about one minute, then it suddenly just blew up. Those two have never liked each other, but . . .'

'It must be the heat,' I said. 'And the smell . . .'

'And the flies,' he said. 'Those bloody flies. Great fat things, and they keep on landing on your face.'

'Flies? We haven't had flies much here . . .'

'Then just thank God for it. They're driving us mad, down the far end. We're changing the pumping crew daily now . . .' He looked at me unbelievingly, and then at where the police were leading Rogers away. 'That man has lost his job, and he's probably going to prison. And all for what? A box of sandwiches. It's mad . . . mad.' Then he walked away back to his remaining crew, head down.

Two idle, hot, bickering hours later, the Bomb Disposal Squad turned up and walked out on the ladders to the bomb. They didn't hang about. We heard distant police loudspeakers telling people to open all their windows, then they blew it up with a small, controlled explosion. We watched from the road, well back. There was a lovely tall spout of mud, out there in the middle, and a nice little bang, but we never heard of any windows reported broken.

It was only a very small bomb, they said.

Crittenden turned up that evening to take a statement about the firemen. I was having a drink on the flat roof that overlooks my back garden. Of course, my back garden is full of shed, but other back gardens still have trees; and I have a little roof-garden with potted conifers, so it's quite pleasant sitting at my little pub cast-iron table, with four aluminium repro French rococo chairs, from B and Q. I offered him a drink, and he had a lime-juice.

When I had finished making my statement, and he had written it down in painful near-copperplate he said, 'That fireman's in a bad way. It could be a murder charge yet.'

'Bad business.' Why do we always say 'bad business' in that stuffy way?

'I shall be glad when that Pond's finished and done with. Under the sod.'

'It's the heat!' We had just reached that stage of a June scorcher when it starts to cool and you find it a luxury to remember just how hot it's been.

'Anything to do with that Pond, the Super dumps it in my lap, now.'

'Any progress on the . . .' I couldn't quite bring myself to say either 'baby' or 'skeleton'.

'Not much. It was about three months old, they reckon. A well-grown boy-child, from the bones. And they've had a bit of success with that crucifix. It was quite an expensive one, silver. With the maker's mark on it. Belgian. Never sold in this country. Never sold anywhere but Belgium. Not much call for them, I suppose, that size. Except in Roman Catholic countries.'

'Any back records of missing Belgian babies?'

'What do you think?' He sighed, and took a long swig of lime. 'Firm stopped making them crucifixes about six years ago. They made them from 1969 till 1981. Not that that gets us much further. We've done a lot of house-to-house, but Wheatstone's the worst place in the world for that kind of thing. They find the bodies of old ladies who've been dead three months and nobody noticed. Aye well, the fire brigade reckon another week to pump the Pond dry. Roll on.'

'Anything about that murdered bookseller?'

'Only that he was a horrible old man – well-known in the occult world. An acquaintance of Aleister Crowley, I believe.'

He did not leave a happy man.

CHAPTER SEVEN

There was more trouble the following morning. It seemed a different sort at first.

The kid with the van and the adhesive tape round his spectacles was back.

'Gorra bit more stuff for you, squire!' he announced, shuffling into my shop. He had a battered cardboard-box under his arm. He put it on my desk without asking permission, and proceeded to unload a collection of tat. And, what's more, I could tell at a glance that it was dangerous tat. Old square wrist-watches, silver propelling pencils with no lead in them, a battered little silver milk-jug that had once been quite nice, some bracelets and other jewellery, and lastly a dressing-table set with silver-backed hairbrush and mirror. All with a neglected look; downright dirty.

It had 'burglary' written all over it; the kind of stuff an incompetent burglar would find in five quick minutes of rifling drawers. I looked at him, with a rising feeling of rage. Everything about him spoke of his incompetence. His mended glasses, the rusty skirts of his van, which he hadn't even tried to repair with fibreglass. The one rear tyre I could see was badly worn; the police would have him for that alone. It would not be long, given such incompetence, before he was caught. And then he would grass, to try to cut down his sentence, and I would be had up for receiving stolen goods . . .

'I don't buy this kind of stuff,' I said coldly. 'It's not the sort of stuff I sell. I only deal in big stuff, furniture . . .'

'And model boats . . .' he said, with a sneer. I realized I was standing on very thin ice; if I offended him, he might shop me anyway. Better buy something off him to shut him up; till I could get down to the Duke of Portland at lunch-time and complain to Mossy about him. I reckoned Mossy would not approve of this free-lancing. I reckoned Mossy would skin him alive when he knew. And I knew Mossy was utterly reliable.

The only thing he had that took my fancy was the silver dressing-table set. It would look quite nice, set out on one of my dressing-tables in the shop.

'How much?' I asked, picking up the mirror and brush. They were twentieth century, but decent. Swags and roses and stuff embossed on the back. Dressing-table sets don't change all that much over the years.

'Sixty.'

I shook my head. 'Forty. That's the best I can do.'

'Fifty-five. 'Sa bargain.'

'Forty,' I said. You have to be firm, dealing with the incompetent.

'Fifty?' He was wilting.

'Forty-five,' I said, taking out my wad of notes and letting a few flutter loose on my desk. His eyes followed their fall greedily; he licked his lips. The incompetent are always mesmerized by any manifestation of real actual money.

'Worrabout the rest?'

'Get Mossy to recommend a *real* fence.' His eyes

77

flickered nervously, and he bundled the stuff back into the box and went without a word. Another worried man . . .

Then I forgot about him, as four students lurched into the yard, two of them walking carefully backwards, carrying something very large and very slippery. Followed by Hermione, grinning like a Cheshire cat.

'It's got to be a thousand-pound bomb,' I shouted. 'How kind. How did you know it was my birthday?'

'Wait till you see.'

'You'll have to hose it down in the yard. It's too big for my sinks.'

'It's too big for *you*, full stop, Morgan!' I'd never seen her so triumphant. 'We got it out of the deep mud in the middle. I knew we'd find the best stuff there. Nearer the shore, they'd have rescued it somehow. It must have broken their hearts.'

I could tell it was a ship, from the two tall broken masts that trailed out of the slime. Four funnels too, by the look of it. And all of four feet long. I got the pressure-hose myself.

'Careful,' she said. 'You're dealing with *real* money here.'

I put the pressure on, and cut at the slime with the jet.

Four tall thin brass funnels, black with verdigris. German tin plate is all very well, but real model-builders liked their brass. I lanced the jet downwards, and the white elaborate bridge of an ocean liner peeped out. Glass still in the windows, and a mass of detail, little steering-wheel and engine-room telegraphs. Then, as I swept the hose back, a row of white lifeboats in authentic working davits, a row of bulging brass ventilators. Finally, the name on the stern: *Olympic.*

'Sister ship of the *Titanic*,' said Hermione. 'Only she never got famous because she never sank.'

I cleared the rear hatch then; reached down and eased back the little brass hooks and pulled it gently off. As the jet reached inside, slime boiled out like an erupting volcano.

'Look at those engines,' said James in an awed tone. 'Scale-model triple-expansion engines. And that boiler, pressure gauges . . . There's a maker's name-plate . . . Ross and Makepeace again.'

'What Bassett-Lowke were to model railways,' said Hermione, 'Ross and Makepeace were to model ships. Make anything for anybody, if you had the money. Retired admirals . . . heads of shipping lines . . . Samuel Cunard . . .'

'Rich men's toys,' I said. 'Not *children's* toys.'

'Oh no, Morgan,' said Hermione, in a very offensive voice. 'You're not getting your hands on *this*.'

'I only meant . . .'

'I know what you meant. If this is sold, the money's going to the museum. And I'm not giving you any commission, either.'

'I see. You want to use my workshop like you own it, but when it comes to something really valuable . . .'

Suddenly we were yelling at each other. Really screaming. Everyone else stared at us in increasing embarrassment.

She dropped her head and shook it savagely, as if she was trying to shake every idea she had out of it. Then she looked up and said with an effort, 'Sorry. I'm being unreasonable.'

I said, matching her sudden calm, 'I'll just get it hosed down completely, then get it inside and get the driers on to it.'

'Thank you,' she said, almost humbly. But I could still sense the rage smouldering inside her.

And inside me, too.

But she turned up that evening, with a bottle of bubbly. And the rage was gone.

'Sorry, Morgan!' The look on her face, I couldn't help forgiving her. And she looked so lovely.

'Come to gloat over your gorgeous find?' I asked, reaching for my keys.

'No,' she said quite sharply. 'We'd probably only start quarrelling over it again. I've had enough quarrelling for one day.'

'Come into my roof-garden, Maude!'

We sat out in the cool, at peace with each other. Finally she said, 'It's not yours, and it's not mine. It still belongs to the family it was made for. Some of them may still be alive.'

'By the laws of marine salvage, they have the right to it, but they, or their insurance company, will have to pay you full current value . . .'

'Or what it cost in . . . when do you think it was made, Morgan?'

'About 1913, I reckon. I expect people liked to be in the fashion, with the new ship – the real *Olympic*, I mean. And I should think certainly before the Great War – surely a firm like Ross and Makepeace would be put on to munitions . . .'

'I don't know. Privilege dies hard . . . we don't know very much at all, do we Morgan? We don't even know for sure that a park lake counts for the laws of marine salvage. Or even whether it applies to scale models. Anyway, how do we trace the owners? Notice in *The Times*?'

'Perhaps through the makers . . .'

'They must have been gone for donkey's years. I never heard of them, even as a girl.'

'I don't know . . . some firms survive. You remember that awful fighter-plane in the Second World War – the Boulton Paul Defiant? Well, the firm of Boulton and Paul still exists – they make metal buildings for farmers . . .'

'As long as I don't have to fly in them . . .'

'No, seriously. You remember the Mitsubishi Zero fighter that gave us so much trouble in the War – same Mitsubishi that makes cars now. There was a Messerschmitt bubble car in the Fifties – I even came across a Heinkel electric gas lighter the other day.'

'Have you got a phone book?' she asked, without much hope.

'Your every wish is my command,' I said gallantly, handing it to her.

'R . . . RO . . . ROSS. Yes, it's here!' Her voice rose to a squeak of excitement. 'Ross and Makepeace, scientific instruments. Morgan, Morgan, let's ring them up, first thing tomorrow!'

But first thing in the morning, I had the Silver Man. I mean, I think his name was Bibby, or Biddle, or something, but all the dealers I knew just called him the Silver Man. He was not, of course, at all silver in colour. A more ordinary bloke you never saw. Tallish, thinnish, bit of a paunch, bald head, small black moustache, and hardly a word out of him, ever. But he came round every week or so, looking in all the antique shops for silver and silver plate, nothing else. A man in a hurry. He would be in and out of your shop in less than five minutes. If he wanted something you had, he'd simply put it on your desk and start counting out the money. He never asked for anything off the price; he simply assumed he would get a ten per cent discount on anything, and of course he got it. He was the only dealer I knew who never stopped to ask how trade was, or moan about it, like every other dealer does. A real hard-working pro; no time for gossip. Somebody told me he lived near Birmingham and covered the whole country once a month. Somebody else said he worked from home; no shop; he shipped everything off to America or the Continent. They said he was worth a bomb; but he always wore the same grey trousers and grey anorak, just this side of respectable.

Now he was studying the dressing-table set, holding it against the light from the window and squinting.

'Quite a nice bit of stuff, that,' I said. 'It's just come in.'

I think he grunted something that might have been 'Belgian'. Then he was dropping the notes on my desk. Then he was gone. I breathed a sigh of relief. It was out of my shop and I felt a bit cleaner and happier. And if the police did turn up, what could I tell them? I hadn't a clue where he lived. Within a week, it'd be gone to America. Out of sight, out of mind. I counted out the sixty pounds in notes he'd left me, and wondered how much he'd get for it, and whether it had been better than I'd thought. But it was a good quick profit of a third, and since it wasn't yet in my stock-book, that took care of any tax and VAT ... the morning seemed brighter, a little.

Then Hermione sailed in, smiling too.

'There's still a Mr Makepeace, and he thinks he can help us,' she said. 'We've got an appointment with him at ten. Want to go and polish your shoes and get respectable?'

'Polish rots the leather,' I said. 'And who's going to look after my shop? I've got a living to make.'

'C'mon, Morgan, where's your sense of adventure? It's me that's taking the risk. I've left Rory in charge. They'll probably dig up the *Queen Mary* today, and drop it under a bus.'

It didn't take long. Ross and Makepeace were in one of those dreadfully boring new factories off the A4, near Slough. We parked in a yard full of containers, Portakabins and dumps of crushed white polystyrene. The entrance was chic, huge red pipes and black Formica, but the other three sides were duller than a cardboard box outside a supermarket. I just knew we weren't going to find anything. We were led through a long workshop full of women in spotless white overalls doing things to lines of matt-black metal boxes. Rows of pale green or red futuristic numbers glowed at us from LCD displays, like the eyes of mad electronic rats.

Mr Makepeace went with his works. He switched on his smile like an LCD display, and shook our hands, ladies first. He must have been over sixty, but you could just tell he played squash three times a week, and had his cholesterol level checked once a month.

Once we had sat down, he announced, 'I know

nothing about this model ship business at all,' and beamed at us through his outsize metal-rimmed spectacles. I mean, what do you say to that?

But the next moment, with another electronic beam, he relented and said, 'It's my father you want. I'm afraid father and I don't see eye to eye about *anything*. But since he's still the principal shareholder in the firm, he has his little way. Or at least, he goes his way and the firm goes mine.' He nodded across his large office, to where there was a door. A door like nothing else in that stainless steel and glass place. It was a very large door, a Georgian door, in dark-red highly-polished mahogany.

And I was pleased also to see a slight tinge of nervousness in that superior stainless smile.

We rose, and knocked on that door gently, and a voice boomed, '*Come*,' and we went into what seemed at first total darkness.

Except there was a coal fire burning, in a glorious heavy oak fireplace; and a couple of old brass and green glass desk-lights switched on, on a huge leather-topped desk. There were modern windows, but they were so heavily curtained with red velvet drapes, and the room was so full of cigarette-smoke that the light they gave was dim. The heat in the room was horrific.

A very old man rose slowly to his feet and held out a huge hand. For he was a huge old man, made even bulkier by a Harris-tweed suit. His newly-washed silver hair fell across a tall forehead in a glorious wave. His features were craggy; only the deep setting of his eyes spoke of age.

'Mr Morgan and Ms Studdart? I suppose you like being called Ms? All this modern stuff and nonsense! Sit ye down, sit ye down!'

We settled in comfortably upholstered 1920s desk-chairs.

'Now, what can I do for you?' He lit another cigarette from the stub of the last, with vigorous puffs.

Very carefully, Hermione explained about our find.

'*Olympic*? Serial number 10167? Never thought to hear of *her* again. We only made one, you know. Heard she went to the bottom with all hands, on the Wheatstone Pond! Run down by some young fool in a rowing-boat . . . Wasn't looking where he was going, eh?' He went into a paroxysm of coughing, ending up by disposing of something into a huge white handkerchief in a very business-like way.

Then he said, 'You want to sell her, of course? We'll give you a fair market price for her. Just glad to get her back, after all these years.' He gave a gesture with a huge hand, and suddenly I saw what was on the walls.

Huge glass cases. Huge model ships inside.

'Thirteen thousand models we made in all. In nearly a hundred years. Not bad going, eh? The First War half killed us, and the Second War finished us off. No money to pay for quality after that – the Americans bled this country dry, you know. Bled us dry. Didn't start Lease-Lend till we were flat stoney broke. Now all we make is damned black boxes. Thirteen thousand models, and in a lifetime I've got back twenty-seven of them. Where's the rest, eh, eh? Tell me that. One comes up at Christie's, from time to time . . . we always get them, in the end. Getting very pricey, though, now. No craftsmanship left in the world, you see.'

Hermione asked who the *Olympic* had belonged to.

'I've looked it up in the records. Chap called

Hutchinson – Samuel Hutchinson. Thirty-nine Belvoir Road, Wheatstone. Called his house 'Nevsky Villa' for some reason best known to himself. Lot of stuff and nonsense! Nevsky Villa indeed! He was a member of the Neptune Yacht Club, of course. Steam section. We made a lot of ships for the Neptune. Bigger and better all the time. Had to do each other down, you see. Great rivalry. Expense no object. Far more money than sense, really. Still, *we* did well out of it. Here they are, damned idiots.'

He passed across a large group photograph. By the Wheatstone Pond (you could tell it by the stone kerbing) a row of trestle-tables had been laid out. Upon them, rows of huge, magnificent steam models. The *Olympic*, in all the glory of shining brass funnels, was among them. There was an even bigger model of a steam-yacht, with a single huge brass funnel. And a model of the *Dreadnought* battleship, and a Mississippi paddle-steamer, tugs, trawlers, cargo-steamers.

Behind this, a row of solemn-faced schoolboys, each with a huge floppy cap on his head, with a button on top, and his small hand on one particular model. And behind each boy, a portly father, moustached or bearded, bewaistcoated, bewatch-chained. Full of civic pomp. On a small blackboard below had been chalked:

Neptune Yacht Club, Steam Section, 1913

'That was almost the last photograph they had taken. Just before the blood-letting started in France. We did a lot of work for the sailing section, too. More sense to that. *They* raced each other – new modifica-

86

tions every year, to sail faster. But the steam section was pure showing off. Couldn't even race the things properly . . . Now *that* model of the *Dreadnought* we do have. Made a dozen of those . . .'

Two hours later, our heads spinning with technical detail, and our lungs fuzzy with fag-smoke, we took our leave and departed, with profuse thanks.

'Come again, any time. You'll find me here. Nowhere else to go to. World's full of damned young women, constantly nagging me about smoking. As if it would make any difference at my age . . .'

'Samuel Hutchinson, 39 Belvoir Road,' said Hermione thoughtfully, as we walked back to the car.

I thought about Abbeywalk being in Belvoir Road as well: but guilty feelings kept me silent.

'Eighty years ago,' I said. 'World's full of Hutchinsons, I'll bet.'

'I'll put adverts in *The Times* and *Telegraph* personal columns. It might do some good.'

'He was ready to do a deal with you on the spot; twelve thousand quid. *He* wouldn't have asked any questions . . .'

'Unlike you, Morgan, I happen to have a conscience.'

We had lunch at a pub I know, on the way home. Gave us time to get over Mr Makepeace; try to work out how old he was.

'He was away at school before the First World War,' I said to Hermione. 'That makes him at least eighty-two.'

'And the rest. Still got all his marbles, though.'

'An old stag at bay. I liked that. They won't shove *him* into any old people's home . . .'

'Probably end up running it, if they did. Didn't like the son much . . .'

'The son's made of plastic and the father's made of oak.'

'Why, Morgan, you have got a poetic soul after all! When money's not involved.'

We drove home in a high good humour. Innocent lambs to the slaughter.

The smell hit us, as soon as we arrived home and opened the car doors. It seemed ten times worse. Really evil.

'Look at the stuff they're pumping out now. They must be very near the end . . .'

The gutters were clogged with black slime. Fresh waves moved downhill like treacle, then gave up moving, leaving a fresh layer. It was more like lava from a volcano than water. Holding our noses, we walked round to the workshop. It seemed abnormally quiet.

'Hallo?' I called.

There was a feeble greeting from the back, and none other than Lenny emerged from behind a row of wardrobes, with a clean yellow duster and a tin of polish in his hands. How often had I told him not to put on polish with clean yellow dusters? I buy rags for that.

'Oh, so you've come back, then?'

He shuffled, eyes on the ground. He didn't look at all well, all pale and sweaty, so I didn't nag him.

'Where's James? And Sam?' Turn your back for five minutes and the idle sods are costing you wages for nothing . . .

'Gone up to the Pond. They came and said there was something else. In the middle . . .'

'I'll give them "in the middle" . . .'

But Hermione said, 'We'd better get up there, Jeff.'

Something was up indeed. Every available ladder led out to the very lip of the deep part, where the firemen were still pumping. There, a veritable island of wooden pallets had been built, and there were about fifteen people standing on it.

'For God's sake,' said Hermione, 'they've built it too close. If it starts to slip into the deep part . . .' We began hurrying along the ladders.

'What the hell's going on?' shouted Hermione as she arrived. 'Rory?'

Rory emerged from the huddle, wearing only bathing-trunks, with a rope round his waist.

'Something big down there.' He pointed.

The edges of what I shall always think of as the pit sloped down at an angle of about forty degrees on all sides. It must have been a hundred feet across, and about thirty feet deep. The bottom was still full of black water, with the armoured hoses of the fire brigade dropping down into it, and pulsing, as the pumping went on. It all looked about as safe as a warm jelly on a plate; a nasty black jelly nobody would ever want to eat. But there *was* something down there on the edge of the water, and it was big; about as big as a man. Or a coffin. As we craned over to look, the island of pallets trembled.

'Everybody off,' said Hermione decisively. 'Except Rory. Go on. *Move!*'

Reluctantly, people began retreating along the ladders, taking two coils of rope with them. It felt a lot safer, once they'd gone. But they were damned reluctant to go. Every face was avid, cheated, angry.

'What the hell are you up to, Rory?'

'Going down. On a rope. Tie the other rope round that thing. Haul it up.' He could hardly get the words out; he was beside himself with the same mad avid excitement.

Hermione pondered; looked at the slope of slime. How stable was it? She picked up a long pole somebody had left, and poked at it. Again, the island of pallets trembled, and I was sure she would call the whole crazy scheme off. But, somehow, the excitement seemed to be seeping into her too, now.

Still, she took her time; consulted the leading fireman from the fire brigade; had more ropes fetched. In the end, we all had ropes round our waists: her, me, and two round Rory. And they all led back to little teams of students, safety aground on the dried-out parts of the mud. I still thought what we were doing was mad; but somehow I no longer cared. I suppose the excitement was undermining *my* common sense too . . .

'Right,' she said at last. 'Down you go, then. And be careful.'

Careful? He stepped cautiously off the island, and immediately the slime sucked him in almost to the top of his thighs. And began to move down the slope with him.

We made frantic hand-signals, and the teams hauled on his ropes. I thanked God as he was pulled clear, as a black treacly avalanche slowly oozed to the bottom of the pit, half burying the long object.

'That'll do,' said Hermione, very finally. 'Whatever it is, it's not worth risking your life for!'

But Rory, far from being scared, was pointing and jabbering, a comic figure, top-half pale white, bottom-half greeny black.

'Bricks, look. Bricks!'

And he was right. Now the avalanche of ooze had fallen, a slope of old brickwork was visible. Glistening under blackness, but still solid brickwork. Some sort of sump or drainhole, put in before the Pond was first flooded.

'It's safe now!' yelled Rory. 'A good foothold all the way down.'

It was a long time before Hermione said anything. She was biting at her lips with anxiety. Impatient shouts came echoing at her from the gangs on the dried mud. I think if they hadn't shouted at her, she might have said no, and everything would have been different. So very, very different.

But in the end she nodded and said, 'One more try.'

He climbed down the slope of brick backwards, looking up at us from time to time, digging his toes into the cracks like a mountaineer. He reached the bottom without mishap, and waded thigh-deep into the slime again, to reach the object. It was a nasty moment. But he sank no deeper once it had reached his waist. After what seemed an eternity of fiddling about, he managed to get one of the ropes round it. I remember he shouted up at us, 'It *is* a boat.'

We signalled, and they began to haul on the rope he'd got round the boat. Slowly, easing the rope as it inched across the pallets, we began to pull it up the bricks. All our eyes were on it; as it boomed out metallically every time it banged on the bricks. The slime was wearing off it; soon the bricks would be doing damage to it . . .

At last, it came up over the lip of the pit; over the edge of the pallets. That was a nasty moment, because the pallets began to slide towards the pit. Then stopped.

I don't know what made me glance down at Rory then; but something did.

The slime had risen up to his chest, and he hadn't even noticed himself . . .

I yelled a warning, and watched him vanish another inch . . .

There was some misunderstanding among the gangs holding the ends of the ropes. It was the ones holding the end of Hermione's rope who pulled; she was dragged over and back across the mud.

The raft of pallets slid down a little more. It was poised directly above poor Rory's upturned face. Another second it would slide in and bury him.

I felt the rope tighten round my own waist. Fools, fools! I clung on to the pallets, and that stopped them sliding for a moment.

And then, thank God, they were pulling on the correct rope; I saw it tighten.

Hermione came back across the pallets; they trembled and began to slide yet again.

But, slowly, the rope round Rory was working. Four inches of his chest reappeared, black with slime . . . then another four inches. But one pallet broke loose and went tumbling down on top of him; he put up his arms to protect himself, but it hit him a nasty thud, and then he was no longer looking up at us, but lolling head-down, under the bulk of the pallet.

'Heave! Heave!' Hermione was screeching now.

Nothing seemed to happen for a long time, and then suddenly the pallet reared up on end and fell away from Rory, and I saw he was out of the mud as far as his thighs. But still inert, unconscious, and worse, face-down.

Another heave, and he was out of it to his knees. But the slimy bricks were scraping at his unprotected face.

'*My* rope – slack off – slowly,' shouted Hermione. And then she was clawing her way down the bricks.

It was the bravest thing I ever saw. I could not have done it in a million years.

As she went, the pallets moved uneasily a fourth time.

But she reached him in the end. I saw her pale face contort with effort, as she slowly, agonizingly, slipping herself all the time, turned him over on to his back.

Then it was me shouting, 'Heave, heave!'

Half-way up, his rope caught between two pallets. Frantically I kicked at them to free it. And all the time the pallets slid and trembled.

Then, of their own accord, nothing to do with me, the pallets shifted again, and his rope was free.

'Heave, heave!' I noticed the brawny firemen were running across the dry mud to join in now.

We got them up at last. Rory's face was a ghastly mask of slime and blood, slowly drying and cracking. But Hermione bent to him and said, 'He's still breathing.'

I felt the island of pallets give a last ominous shift.

'Look out. It's going.'

Then we were off them and wading through knee-high mud, dragging poor Rory between us.

Behind, I heard the clatter as the pallets fell to their doom.

The ambulance had gone with Rory. He was still breathing, and even had his eyes open. And they'd washed the mud and blood off his face, and said he wasn't bleeding seriously anywhere, but perhaps there might be internal injuries. He certainly wasn't saying anything to anybody; just giving convulsive shivers.

Of the pallets which had been on the edge of the pit, there was no sign. Gone under the mud. And the outermost of our ladders had gone with them, too.

But something still lay, large and bulky, on the edge of the pit. The model ship that Rory had nearly lost his life for. It was still on the end of the last rope; the rope had saved it. We all stared at it, with very mixed feelings. I think, left to myself, I would have left it there. But one of the students said, 'We might as well have it. Rory will want to see it, when he comes out of hospital.'

'C'mon, lads, one last heave-ho for good old Rory.'

Two of them approached it along the ladders, *very* cautiously. They guided it with their outstretched hands, while the rest of us pulled. Then, when it finally reached the dried-out mud, six of them went out, put it on their shoulders, and carried it to shore.

Was it only me that thought they looked like pall-bearers with a coffin?

But of course, close-to, it was nothing like a coffin. Coffins don't have single masts at the front, and propellers at the stern. Keep hold of your sick imagination, Morgan!

And so they carried it into my workshop and laid it

on two trestles. And then discovered it was nearly six o'clock and as somebody said wryly, 'Doesn't time pass quickly when you're enjoying yourself?'

So they all dispersed, longing for showers, and vowing to ring up the hospital to find out how good old Rory was. Left alone, I gave the thing one look and shivered. I locked up, saying it could wait till I'd had a good night's sleep.

I did not have a good night's sleep. I had nightmares, and wakened sweating a dozen times.

But, oddly, not nightmares about mud or death, or poor old Rory choking under the slime.

No: nightmares about Hermione Studdart, who I was pursuing through a dark wood.

Hermione Studdart, who I was going to rape. And kill.

CHAPTER EIGHT

I was a long time getting up next morning. I went and got a mug of coffee and smoked several fags, sitting on my bed and rubbing my eyes and scratching my head and surveying parts of my body I was not very satisfied with, in the hopeless hope that they had mysteriously improved overnight. The nightmares were very hard to shake off. They shocked me, and horrified me, and yet I kept on coming back to them, like your tongue does to the gap when you've had a tooth out. I mean, I'd never even considered rape, in all my life. I like women. And I've always thought that what is not freely given by them is of no value anyway. Seducers are not usually rapists; different breed. And yet the feminists say all men are rapists at heart . . .

Finally I came to the conclusion that if I didn't make a real effort to get moving, I'd sit there all day. Normally I find that each thing I do, washing, shaving, even putting on my wrist-watch, jerks me a little nearer to coping with the day. But not that morning. The temptingly terrified fleeing ghost of Hermione was with me in the bathroom, over breakfast . . .

Oh, for God's sake get among some real people, Morgan!

I decided to drop in to the Duke of Portland. It was always rather nice and quiet, before the pre-lunch mob dropped in. I'd buy an *Observer* on the way and . . .

Mossy Hughes saw me the moment I poked my head round the swing-door.

'Mr Morgan. What you havin'? Guinness Bitter, innit?' He smiled, pleased with himself for remembering. Fetched the two pints to a sunlit corner-table.

'Can't beat Sunday, can you, Mr Morgan? Day o' rest. Good enough for Gawd, good enough for me, is what I say.'

'Very true, Mossy,' I said, as solemnly as if I was in church. While the ghost of Hermione Studdart shrank back in pleading terror as her blouse tore beneath my hand. Still, it was fading now, thank God. Another five minutes, I'd be rid of it. I hoped I could keep my conversation sensible until then.

'You get that boat OK, Mr Morgan?'

'Yes . . . thanks. He brought me two more from the same place. A tug and a lightship. They must have belonged to Tony Tanner too. I gave him a fair price . . .'

'Oh, he did, did he? Just forgot to tell me about it! I'll have a word wi' that young man! He's a bit too fond of making a bit on the side!'

'Well . . .' I hesitated. I did not want to make trouble, but . . .

'Been up to something else, has he?'

I told him about the tat.

'You didn't take anything off him?' Mossy's concerned face peered into mine.

I told him about the dressing-table set. His forehead creased into its usual frowns. 'How much you give him?' Then he got to his feet and said, 'I'll have a word wi' that young man,' and went straight off to the phone booth in the entrance-hall. Then he came

97

back and said, 'He's coming round now, *tout de suite*. I'm going to have to sort him out afore he gets into real trouble.'

Then he drew heavily on his pint and said, 'The young's a great problem, these days, Mr Morgan. The old rules don't mean nothing to them. I give him a straight simple job to do, but can he do it? No, he has to have ideas of his own. If it wasn't for his mother's sake, I'd have kicked him out years ago. He'll be the end of me. But his mother won't hear a word agin him.'

I just drew on my own pint with a sage nod. Mossy's relationships I did not wish to go into . . .

Finally, the youth came in, saw us and threw himself into a chair at our table, with a look of sullen nervousness on his face that made me want to kick him.

'A tugboat an' a lightship,' said Mossy heavily. 'Thanks for telling me, Spud.' The youth gave me a look of frank dislike, but otherwise said nothing.

'And I hear you've been bothering Mr Morgan here with some of your own rubbish.'

'Weren't rubbish.'

'Let me tell you something, son. Mr Morgan here's a *friend* of mine. A good friend. An' I don't want my friends *bothered*. Right? Now where'd you get that stuff? Police looking for it?'

'Nah,' said the youth. 'Came from the same place, dinnit? Them old suitcases. Went back after and had a look in them. Weren't much . . .'

Mossy relaxed. 'That's all right then. It's not dodgy, Mr Morgan. It won't cause you no trouble.'

But, on the contrary, a vague unease was niggling at the back of my mind. 'That suitcase you got the dressing-table set from . . . what else was in it?'

'Just some tart's stuff. Ponged horrible. Foreign tart.'

'Why do you say foreign?'

'There were some letters . . . mebbe in French. Not in English, anyway. French . . . French letters!' He grinned, as if he had made some superb joke. Nobody except him found it funny.

'What else?'

'Oh, bras an' stuff. A couple of books in French. And some kid's stuff . . .'

'Like what?'

'Oh, bootees, little cardigans.'

The skin over my spine crept. Right there, in that warm sunny pub, I came out in goose-pimples.

Mossy gave me a worried look. 'Was she a friend of yours, Mr Morgan?' Oh, how many relationships can the word 'friend' cover?

'No,' I said. 'But I'd like to have a look in that suitcase sometime.'

Mossy jerked his head at the youth. 'You heard what Mr Morgan said . . .'

'What, now? In broad daylight?'

'For Gawd's sake,' said Mossy. 'Shove on a long brown coat. Hold a clipboard in yer hand. Tell anybody who asks you're from the council investigating a complaint about rats . . . use yer bloody loaf. Go on, get moving. We haven't got all bloody day. And fer Gawd's sake bring the right bloody suitcase.'

I glanced around the public bar nervously. But no one was taking a blind bit of notice of us. All too busy talking, swanking about the next car they were going to buy. Or how they were going to make a killing, once business improved . . . still, it was an uneasy half-hour, before the youth came back and jerked his head towards the door.

'In the back of the van.'

'Let's go then.'

We left one of the back doors of the tattered van half open, for light. I knelt and undid a leather strap. The two heavy brass catches on the suitcase thumped back against the leather with reports like a gun going off. Mossy's eyes watched me, in the gloom. Curious, genuinely worried for me and yet . . . discreet.

The odour of woman's stuff was still strong, but gone sour, stale. Among the rumpled female garments, something glass showed. I pulled it out.

A baby's feeding-bottle. Unwashed. Still with some pale green sediment in the bottom. And there were the little bootees, grubby, unwashed. Some bits of white terry-towelling, that on closer examination turned out to be nappies. A dried-out bottle of gripe-water.

Books. Paperbacks that I could see at a glance were French. With lurid covers that showed women oddly dated in their clothing. A cheap copy of *La Récherche du Temps Perdu*, Thérèse Raquin . . .

Then a tiny, dark book with hard-bound covers, but no title. I flicked open the pages. A small diary, with a week to two pages, covered in tiny writing, full of what seemed to be abbreviations. It didn't matter, I couldn't read French anyway. Gave it up in the third year and did art instead.

And then the letters; on cheap paper, in cheap envelopes, that didn't look English. All addressed in a big sprawling hand that was not the hand that had written the diary. And all addressed to the same address:

Mlle Annette le Feuvre
19 Neville Road
Golders Green
Londres
Angleterre

A foreign unmarried mother. And the dates on the envelopes were ten years old. And the postmark was 'Liège'.

Belgian. Like the dressing-table set.

Like the crucifix inside the tiny coffin. Again, in my mind's eye, the tiny skull peered out at me.

'Dodgy, Mr Morgan?'

I gave a warning sideways glance at the boy, who was squatting, idly picking his nose.

'Go an' get me a packet o' fags, Spud!'

With ill grace, the youth leapt out of the van. He knew he was being got rid of, and resented it. We listened while his footsteps faded.

'*Very* dodgy, Mossy,' I said. 'When we were searching the Pond, we turned up a baby's body . . .'

He nodded. 'Murdered. Black magic ritual or something. I heard some talk about that.'

'There was a crucifix with the body. The police found out it was Belgian. That dressing-table set he sold me – that was Belgian as well. And this girl's a Belgian unmarried mum . . .'

He shuddered. 'Christ, it's a bloody shitty world, innit? What yer going to do, Mr Morgan?'

I began doing up the suitcase. 'I don't know yet. I think I'd better talk to a friend of mine.'

Of course, the friend was Hermione Studdart.

*

I rang her from the pub. She sounded bright and quite friendly. She said, 'You wondering about Rory? I rang the hospital. He's going to be OK. His face will be a bit of a mess for a while. And they say he's still in shock. I had a long chat with the sister. She was nice.'

'Something else has come up.'

'What?'

'Rather not say, over the phone . . .'

'I'll come round . . .'

I felt a sudden irrational reluctance to go home. Maybe it was shame. Maybe I didn't want the real Hermione waltzing through my dreams of rape. 'D'you mind if I come to you?'

'*That* serious, is it? Or do you want an excuse to case my joint?' Her voice was still friendly, playful. 'Oh, well, come round if you must. I suppose I can rustle up some coffee. D'you know where I am? It's just off Kensington Church Street; a mews . . . Oh, you brought me home once.'

A nice Georgian mews. And she hadn't wasted space on a garage; her battered Metro lived on the cobbles, and where the stable had been there was a gracious little sitting-room, with cast-iron spiral stair leading up out of it. She had some nice bits of furniture; a Georgian bureau, two spindle-backed armchairs with the pukka curved stretchers . . .

'Don't you *dare* make me an offer! It's all family heirlooms.' She looked cool, relaxed, casual and elegant in dark green slacks and a loose green top. She glanced at the big suitcase in my hand. 'I asked you for coffee – I trust you're not thinking of moving in?'

How could I ever have even dreamt of raping some-one so nice, so civilized, so friendly? And yet, as I put down the suitcase, dark shadows drifted across my mind. And when I opened the suitcase, they got worse, not better.

She knelt beside it, and wrinkled her straight elegant nose.

'You're going down-market like an express train, Morgan.' Then she picked up the bootees with one hand, and one of the letters with the other, pondered for a second, then said, with a face full of distress, 'The baby in the Pond.'

I mean, she was that quick, that intelligent. She added sadly, 'We've had two more little skeletons. But nothing like *that*. Just ordinary dumpings, over the years. But it's very sad, isn't it?' Somehow, the way she said it, I knew she was thinking that she was over thirty, and without a bloke, let alone a baby, in sight. They have it a bit rough, on the quiet, these modern career women. But how could I empathize with her so, with those evil rags of dreams still drifting through my mind?

She spread the girl's pathetic belongings around her hearthrug, gently trying to smooth out the crumplings. Her respect for them began to rebuild a whole human life before my eyes. Gay floral blouses, a white suspender-belt . . . a young and sexy girl, she must have been.

'The letters are in French,' I said lamely. 'And there's a diary . . . *my* French is hopeless. I thought you . . .'

She nodded, and opened a letter.

'*Ma Chère Annette* . . . my dear Annette . . . once again I urge you to come home. Your father . . . has had a change of heart. He is no longer . . . angry. He

103

misses you. I have found a family . . . a good and loving family . . . who will take the baby. They live quite near . . . twenty kilometres . . . you could go and see the child each weekend . . . they are not jealous people. It is so foolish of you . . . to imagine you can make a living in a foreign country, with the burden of a child. I urge you to reconsider . . .'

Hermione looked across at me. 'Not much doubt what happened there . . .'

'So why . . . kill the child?'

She took up the little diary, squinting at it, putting one finger to the outer corner of her right eye, to stretch it and help her vision. 'Oh, God, this is hopeless. It's as if it was written by a demented ant. And it's more than half abbreviations . . . I can't do anything with this, Morgan.'

She turned to the last page. 'Oh, this last bit's bigger and clearer. It says, "They shall have me, but they shall not have him." Was that . . . what we found . . . a boy, Morgan?'

'Crittenden said they reckoned it was.'

We were both silent a long time, while she fingered and rearranged the crumpled clothing, as if in a vain desire to help.

Finally, I blurted out, 'What d'you reckon made her *do* it?'

'How the hell would I know?' Suddenly her face was the harsh ill-tempered face she could show on site, when things were going badly.

Then she seemed to get a grip on herself; and said more gently, almost apologetically, 'Childbirth does strange things to women, Morgan. Sometimes they get very depressed after it. Sometimes they do feel like murdering their babies . . . the strain of looking after them gets too much, and yet they can't bear to hand them over to anybody else. And don't forget she was alone. And probably had no job . . . money running out . . . disapproved of at home. She must have been under a hell of a strain. Under the law, it's called "infanticide", not "murder". The penalties are far less severe; even the law *sort* of understands.'

She shook her head, as if to shake slow, bad thoughts out of it. Then turned to me and said, 'What are you going to do — with this stuff?'

'God knows. I can hardly take it to Crittenden and say, "a clue has turned up to your murder as a result of a burglary."'

'No, I can see you've made difficulties for yourself, with your dodgy dealing.' She even managed a slight wry smile that had some affection in it. 'I suppose . . . it all happened a long time ago. And she wouldn't make a *habit* of murdering babies . . . I doubt if she's a danger to anybody else, wherever she is now, poor thing. I only hope . . . she didn't do away with *herself*.'

That was a new and worrying thought that hadn't occurred to me.

'I could fish around Crittenden a bit . . . after all, I am entitled to an interest in this case, seeing that we found the . . . body,' I said.

'Yes. I'd be interested to hear what he tells you. Did her parents ever report Annette as a missing person? Did she ever turn up?'

Then, quite suddenly and briskly she was packing up the suitcase again. Putting all the dreary frightening thoughts out of her mind. 'I'll make you that coffee now. Always as good as their word, the City Toy Museum . . .'

We felt better after it was packed away. She offered to shove it into her outhouse, for which I was grateful. We felt better still after I'd asked her out to lunch. We got really quite cheerful over lunch. And in Regent's Park afterwards. Our acquaintanceship, I would have said, really began to prosper. At least she was calling me 'Jeff', not 'Morgan'.

I rang Crittenden the following morning, early. He'd just come on duty, I think. He kept breaking off to make sarcastic remarks to his subordinates, as they clocked in.

I started by discussing the vandalism round the site, which had got much less. The kids seemed to be losing interest in us; we had been the usual nine day's wonder. And then, as he made the noises that indicated he was a busy man, and had other things to do with his life, I mentioned the baby from the Pond.

'I just wondered,' I said casually, 'whether you ought to look up Belgian girls in the Missing Persons' file?'

'We did that *days* ago.'

'Any luck?'

'There were *seventeen*, over the three years we covered.'

'Oh!' I said glumly.

'Mind you, thirteen of those turned up alive, eventually. And one dead. Strangled. But we got the bloke who did it.'

'Three left, then?'

'That's what my arithmetic makes it.'

'What were their names?'

He paused, probably to consult his notebook. 'Helene Rigaude, last heard of in Bromley, Kent. Michelle Janviér, reported to have gone with a dance troupe to the Middle East, God help her. And one Annette le Feuvre, complete with baby. The kid was the right age . . . but she last lived over in Golders Green.'

I swallowed hard. 'That one sounds more likely.'

'Why do you say that, Mr Morgan?' There was a sudden sharkish snatching tone in his voice. Policemen can seem like anybody else, for a long time, and then suddenly you get that sharkish tone.

'Well . . . the kid.'

'Yeah, the kid.' His tone returned to its ordinary disillusionment. 'Well, anything turns up, let me know, won't you? Meanwhile, if you will excuse me, London crime is like the busy noise of London traffic. It never stops, day or night.'

I heard James's car pull into the yard soon after that, and knew it was time to get downstairs for the working day. Instead I went to the window and watched James and Sam get out, their hands full of sandwich-boxes, and copies of the tabloids. Sam went in for the *Sun*; James for the more righteous *Mail*. They got into the workshop quickly, because it was beginning to rain, under a dark grey sky. There wouldn't be much activity at the Pond today, if this weather kept up. And not much in my shop, either. Bad selling weather. Best selling weather is a cold sunny day. People are lured out for a walk, then feel the chill and come into the shop for a warm. I keep a good coal fire; it makes people want to linger. I offer coffee to anybody I know; loosens up their buying-spirit.

I had never felt more reluctant to go and face the world. I'd had another night of nightmares; again about raping Hermione. How can you spend a happy day with a woman, and then dream of raping and murdering her? I wondered whether, while I was with her, she dominated me, turned me into a good little boy behaving himself for the nice lady . . . and then, after we had parted, the resentment welled back up to the surface, so I dreamt of rape. It seemed as good an explanation as any.

And the Belgian girl was also making me broody . . . and the grey sky. Anyway, I got hold of myself, and went downstairs.

James and Sam were dismantling a grandfather clock I'd sold the previous Friday, to a woman in Hampstead. Sam was going up with it in the van, to set it up for her. If I knew the uneven walls and floors of Hampstead, that would take the whole morning. Sam's a good worker, but he likes to chat the rich ladies up.

'What you on, James?' I asked

'That German box-clock's stopped again. I gave it a squirt of WD40 on Friday, but it hasn't done the trick. Only went about four hours, I reckon. I'll give it an hour in the paraffin bucket and go on from there. And that Dutch chandelier could do with a clean. I like doing brass on a rotten day. Cheers me up.' He looked at the new model boat from the Pond, with less than enthusiasm. 'You gonna get that thing hosed down outside? We could do with its room, and without its stink.'

'Young Lenny can do it, when he finally turns up.'

'Here he is now,' said Sam, 'looking like a wet Sunday.'

James gave him a sharp look, for making rude remarks about Sunday. Sam at least *pretended* to be an atheist; mainly, I guess, to annoy James and to while away many a boring hour with argument.

I must admit young Lenny looked pretty ghastly; very pale, and jumpy. And very slow to give us a hand with the boat. It was a handful for four, and it didn't help that the slime on it had dried on the surface, like the top of a cow-pat, but underneath was still wet and greasy, so that your hands slid on crumpling patches of the dried stuff. It was damned heavy, too; full of silt. Worse, three of us had to stand holding it, while Lenny nipped back for the trestles; and didn't he take his time?

'Yeuk!' Sam made a noise of disgust, deep in his throat, flapped his hands to try to shake the slime off them, and dived for the wash-basin, where he spent about ten minutes washing them. Then he went off, and James spent about ten minutes washing *his* hands. Was no one going to make a start this morning? But the stuff *was* unpleasant. It tightened on your skin as it dried, gave the delusion of burning the skin, like paint-stripper ... I spent a long time washing in turn, making sure it was out of every crack and crevice ... I thought it was odd at the time.

Then I decided to follow James's example, and polish every bit of brass in my shop. The doorstops in the form of charging hussars were rather fun, every detail of sword and cross-belts coming up beautifully. But the grain-measures (set of three) were a boring drag ...

Then Lenny darkened the doorway; he seemed to have got himself pretty wet, even though it wasn't yet raining more than a spot. He would hardly ever wear an apron for a dirty job, like the older men. I supposed he had a daft mother who spent endless hours washing his ragged jeans.

'Done the outside of it,' he said sullenly.

'So?' I said, tempted to be nasty in return.

'Thought you would want to see it.'

'Oh, all right!' Where had all the enthusiasm gone, that had made us gather so avidly round the first little German tin-plate cruiser? I suppose you can get sick of handling gold and jewels in the end, if you have enough of them . . .

It was certainly a fine model ship; a very expensive model ship. A white hull, faintly spotted all over with green algae, six feet long and a foot across. Finely-fitted deck planking, beautifully-cast brass handrails, a varnished wooden superstructure, not even beginning to rot, a white bridge, brass ventilators, all dominated by a single fat brass funnel. The glass in the windows was even bevelled, and quite perfect. And there was the brass-maker's plate, which I knew must say 'Ross and Makepeace' even before I looked at it.

I turned the six-inch steering-wheel on the bridge, and the white rudder swung; I moved the handles of the engine-room telegraphs. Everything was made to *work*. Extraordinary.

So was the engine-room, under the hatch that Lenny had lifted off at the back. Brass feed-tanks for the methylated spirit, little pipes leading down to the burners. No chance that this one would catch fire in mid-voyage. Little working pressure-gauges, and the mini ature triple-expansion engine was a masterpiece of engineering, in brass, nearly a foot long and a foot high.

Oh, this was out of this world! The ultimate dream of a model boat! This was one that Christie's or Sotheby's would probably send to New York! A hundred thousand dollars? Two hundred thousand? The sky was the limit, once the millionaire yachtsmen got their eyes on it.

And yet all I felt was a dull hate for the thing. It was too big, too overblown. It wasn't really a model at all. When things get too big, they cease to be models for me. Like that model of a Cunarder, ten feet long, in Liverpool Museum. You can admire it, but you can't relate to it. A bloke could have sat on the deck of this thing, and it would have carried him around the lake, with his feet trailing in the water. What made it worse was that the real ship it was copied from couldn't have been more than sixty foot long, the smallest kind of steam-yacht. I lost interest, beyond thinking that Hermione was going to make a lot of money. And once I thought of Hermione, those rotten rape-dreams came back like a dull toothache.

'All right,' I said, 'get the front end cleaned out.' There was a long hatch over the bows, with a glass roof; but you couldn't see inside what must be the saloon; the glass was all misted.

'Can't seem to find the catches,' whined Lenny. 'Can't get the top off.'

'Well, *look* for them.' I went back to cleaning my brass.

I was still polishing the last grain-measure when I heard him start screaming.

*

III

I'd heard screaming like it, once or twice. Once after a road accident, and once when one of my blokes got a faceful of Nitromors because some other fool was messing about. You don't hang about when you hear that kind of screaming. You *run*.

My first feeling was one of relief. Lenny was just standing there, looking down into the boat. He still seemed to have both arms and legs; and eyes. He wasn't bleeding; he still clutched the hose in one hand, though it was dumping all its water on his already-sodden shoes and jeans.

I went up and grabbed him. I suppose to reassure him, and to make him stop. But he didn't stop. It was as if he was having some kind of fit. What the . . .

I looked down to where his gaze was immovably fixed. He had the glass hatch on the bows off, and you could look down inside. Again, the inside was beautifully finished. Red upholstered miniature benches, with mahogany locker doors underneath.

The red upholstery was dark and sodden, as you would have expected.

The horror was on the upholstery. Three things, huddled together, as if for mutual protection. Tied down by a glistening membrane of gunge.

Three tiny skeletons, the middle one a bit bigger than the others, still with rags of clothing around them. Skeletons about a foot high, perfect in their tiny, thin detail, like the skeletons of starlings that fall down the chimney when you have the sweep.

Only these skeletons were undoubtedly human.

I heard, far off as in a daze, Lenny stop screaming and take to his heels and run from my yard. I never saw

112

him again. One night, much later, his mother rang up to ask for his cards. I asked how he was; but his mother wouldn't say anything. She couldn't get off the phone fast enough.

Now I was aware of heavy breathing on my other side.

'Great God Almighty,' said James; and it wasn't a curse, it was a cry for help. Then he said, shakily, 'They must be plastic . . . but damned clever. Damned accurate . . .'

'When this ship went down,' I said, 'plastic hadn't been invented.'

'Ivory, then. You know what the Chinese can do with ivory.'

'There's . . . still . . . bits of muscle . . . attached.' It reminded me of a stripped Sunday chicken you find the following Friday in the back of the fridge. Or the Friday after that.

And it smelt like it, too. I suddenly turned away, and threw up all over the cobbles of the yard.

I heard James say, dully, to himself, 'Monkey-skeletons. Baby monkeys . . . what a filthy trick. Drowning baby monkeys like that.'

It sort of made the world all right. Unbearably nasty, yes, but still sane. I turned to look again, with hope. Then I said flatly, 'They're not monkeys; I've seen plenty of monkey-skulls. These skulls are too small. The hands and feet are too small for monkeys.'

'What are they then. Human foetuses?'

'Don't be stupid. Foetuses have *huge* heads.'

There was a long silence. Then he said, as if he were defending his beloved faith with his life itself, 'It's a trick. A filthy trick. Someone with a mind like a sewer.' And he turned and stumbled back to the workshop; then I heard him being sick, too.

Footsteps. Light female footsteps. I desperately tried to get the hatch-cover back on, but I was blind and fumbling; it caught the brass rail and fell to the cobbles with a sound of breaking glass.

'Jeff, *careful*,' said Hermione crossly. Bent down to pick up the hatch, and *saw*.

She didn't scream. She caught herself in time and didn't scream.

I'll always admire her for that.

We sat in my office, and drank whisky. Normally, I wouldn't touch whisky with a barge-pole. I hate the stuff. But in dreadful moments it's a help. It's as bitter as death itself; it burns your throat and masks the other pain.

I drink a lot of whisky at funerals.

When I say I was drinking whisky, that sounds a bit too elegant. I was holding a full glass with both hands and both hands were shaking, and the whisky was slopping over them. And my lips felt huge and rubbery, and full of subtle little movements out of my control. It was just like when I heard my father had been killed. Only worse.

'It's a trick,' said James for the hundredth time. 'A vile trick.' I felt like hitting him. Why couldn't he think of something else to say?

'Jeff,' said Hermione, in a very small voice, 'it *could* be a trick, you know. The Victorians were always pulling tricks. Think about Piltdown Man – what a hoax he was. Human skull, ape's jaw.'

Some detached part of my mind insisted she'd got it the wrong way round. That Victorian gent had used an ape's skull and a human jaw . . . but that little part of myself would never connect with my mouth, would never be heard out loud. It was just a little voice inside my head . . .

'We need *experts*,' said Hermione.

'You mean, dial 999?' I asked, with a burst of black savagery. 'Get Crittenden round? He'd take one look and sniff, and send the Social Services round for *us* – to take us to the nearest bin. Crittenden only likes life-size skeletons, and he doesn't do an awful lot about *those*.'

'I think you underestimate Crittenden,' she said quietly.

So why did I feel like murdering her?

'Pygmies,' said James to himself. 'Young pygmies. Skeletons of young pygmies.'

'Pygmies,' I snarled, 'are nearly five feet tall. I've seen them on the telly.'

'Them head-hunters in Borneo. They shrink human heads . . .'

'They take the skull *out* before they shrink them.'

'Bits of all sorts of animals, put together . . . a rabbit's thigh-bone looks like a little human thigh-bone . . .'

'He's right, you know, Jeff,' said Hermione. 'We could be having hysterics over *nothing*. We've got to get some experts.'

'You want a taxidermist,' said James. 'They know bones. Or some doctor as can keep his mouth shut.'

Somehow, that made me think of Mossy Hughes. I somehow knew he would know a doctor who would keep his mouth shut. Maybe he would know a taxidermist who would keep his mouth shut, too.

I rang the Duke of Portland and they fetched Mossy

straight away. I supposed that now they served pub grub, he must never go home at all.

'What can I do for you, squire? A taxidermist who can keep his mouth shut? You wanna get stuffed, on the quiet?'

Somehow I could not rise to the occasion.

'An' a doctor who can keep his mouth shut? That'll cost ya. What you done, got wounded burgling the Natural History Museum?' But his voice was worried now. 'You're in real trouble, squire, ain't ya? Can I help? I can come round straight away . . .'

I thought that, from him, was a very generous offer. And somehow, God knew how, I thought he would be a help. There was an air about Mossy of having done everything and having seen everything. Just the man for a committee discussing the Impossible, the Unbelievable.

'You get them and bring them along, Mossy. We'll be waiting.'

After that, there was nothing to do but look out of the window at the steadily falling rain. We had done all we could do. With loathing, the three of us had carried the boat into a separate side-shed I seldom used. And locked the big padlock on the door. I had rung the house at Hampstead, where Sam was, and sent him on a long round of the clock repairers of the East End, looking for a second-hand part for a very rare clock. And he could go straight home afterwards.

It was a sort of dull relief, just to sit and wait.

We went back to my office, when they'd finished looking. We gave them whisky, too. Only Mossy, stony-faced, drank his with any sign of pleasure.

The taxidermist raised a pale elderly face. 'They're not the bones of any animal I've ever seen, and I've seen the lot, I think. They're certainly not monkey-bones.'

I put a cheque into his trembling hand, and he went with great relief. I hoped he didn't have a weak heart. At that age, shocks can be deadly. On the other hand, the elderly, the successful elderly, have a way of defending themselves against shocks.

When his footsteps had faded, the doctor cleared his throat. I could tell that he, too, was anxious to be gone. It didn't make me feel any better.

'I think he's right. They have the *feel* of human bones.'

'But *how can* they be human bones?' I felt my last chance of sanity was slipping away with him.

'I have just one thought – and that's from reading, not from experience. In the War – the Hamburg bombing – the fire typhoon. Some of the people who died in the shelters, under the intense heat . . . the rescue squads thought that the bodies of adults were the bodies of very young children, they had shrunk so much . . . but I would think in that case the bones would be very brittle – hard to handle and arrange. They would break very easily.' He got up to go. I reached for my cheque-book again, but he waved his hand, with a look on his face that I think was pity. 'No – no payment. It's not really a criminal matter, though I can see you have a problem. My advice to you is to hand the whole thing – the whole shooting-match – over to the police. Let them deal with it. Let them worry about it. They've got the experts; who will no doubt be utterly fascinated. Good night to you. Thanks, I can find my own way out.'

We listened to his footsteps retreating up to the side entrance. Then James said, 'I'll have to go. The missis will be frantic.'

We listened, through the drawn curtains, to him get into his car and drive away. A cold loneliness seemed to seep into the room, from the locked-up shed where the dead awaited our verdict.

'Not going to stay here on your own tonight, squire?' asked Mossy. I could have hugged him, for his concern.

'No,' said Hermione. 'He's coming home with me.'

CHAPTER NINE

All my later admiration of Hermione stemmed from that night. How could she be so brisk, so efficient? It was only thanks to her that we left my house in good order. It was she who went upstairs to dig out my toothbrush and pyjamas, dressing-gown and razor. It was she who got me into my overcoat and made sure my doors were locked and the burglar-alarms on.

She drove calmly and efficiently. I thought things would be better, once we left my gate. As that old poem says, from my school-days, 'out of sight, out of mind, we'll think of cleaner things'. But you don't, you know. The contents of the saloon of that model ship kept flashing on the screen of my mind over and over, like an obscene slide-show when the projector is stuck.

I tried to draw comfort, a little still comfort from the things we passed; a wet wall glistening in the lamplight, with a spray of bright leaves drooping over it; a man lighting a cigarette on a street-corner, waiting for the lights to change; even the good old London buses, the 82 VICTORIA and the 10 HAMMERSMITH beaming their glowing signs before them.

None of it worked. Everything belonged to a world that had fractured, that had torn like stage scenery to reveal a darkness behind. It was as if Christopher Columbus *had* reached that edge of the world his crew always feared, and seen the water streaming over the edge in some colossal Niagara, to fall for ever as spray among the stars ... But was it the world that was fractured, or me? I still had the same two arms and the same two legs, and lungs that breathed and a heart that pounded and a mind that could think, but what use were they, scattered across the wasteland of that discovery?

It was good to be in her lighted room, to watch her hold a match to the coal-effect gas fire, and draw the curtains. But what was she drawing the curtains *on*? What horror was kept out only by thin glass and thinner cloth?

She knelt on the hearthrug, holding her slim hands to the as yet heatless blaze. How elegant she seemed, now that it no longer mattered, now that nothing mattered. I tried out the doctor's wise words about the Hamburg fire-victims, and found they didn't convince me at all. They would undoubtedly comfort the good doctor, while he forgot the reality, cut it down till eventually it would be no more than an odd experience, a traveller's tale, to be told to a circle of admiring grandchildren, round some fire on a winter's night. How their little eyes would shine with wonder and excitement; removed from the reality by space and time.

I had to live with it. It was locked in my shed.

Finally, Hermione said, not taking her eyes off the flames, 'We have to talk. If we want any sleep to-night.'

And I just said, 'Yes.'

'You don't believe that stuff the doctor said? About Hamburg?'

'No. There was no sign of charring. And I don't believe even fire-victims would shrink *that* small. Besides . . .'

'Don't go on. I don't believe it either.' She gave a delicate shudder. 'And yet . . . we can't deny it has happened. In a real model ship, made by a real firm. We've got to accept that. If we don't . . . I think it will make us ill. We'll never trust anything again.'

'Yes.' It was good to talk; it was good to know that one other person in the world felt the same.

'We've . . . got to move on. If we just sit still, we're *finished*. We've *got* to find out more about it.'

'*How*?' My mind swam hopelessly; I couldn't get a grip on anything.

'Well, obviously, basic research. Starting with Mr Makepeace, in the morning.'

I was aghast. 'He's too old. He wouldn't believe us, but he'd still be terribly shocked. He'd think we were mad. It might give him a heart attack. His beloved ships . . .'

'Oh yes,' she said, quite coolly. 'We can't tell *him* anything. It's what he'll be able to tell us. About his beloved ships. And the Neptune Yacht Club. Steam section.'

It all seemed so . . . trivial. 'I don't see how that's going to help us. *Nothing* we might learn will make this right . . . make sense.'

She looked at me very solemnly, and then I noticed the little tic that made her eyelid flutter, and knew how much her calm was costing her. 'Can you suggest anything better?'

I shook my head hopelessly; and yet I did feel better for having some plan, something useful to do, however trivial.

'I shall ring Sven, and call a halt on the dig. I don't want them around, till this is sorted. I feel responsible for them. Too many things have gone wrong already. Rory; those firemen. You know, I've really hated this dig. Right from the beginning. We've found all those marvellous things, and yet I've felt . . . we're getting deeper and deeper into trouble. You know what I mean?'

I thought of Lenny. Then I began to worry aloud about James and Sam.

'What'll you do with them?' she asked.

'Send them up to Birmingham with the big van, I think. For two or three days. Going round the antique hypermarkets, and house-to-house, on the knocker. James has done it before for me, when stuff's been short. He knows what to look for. And how much to pay. I trust him. It'll get some fresh air into his lungs. I'll give him some bearer cheques on my bank for five thousand, that'll see them through.'

It says a lot for my state of mind that I said five thousand without a thought. Normally five thousand's a lot for me. But at that moment, I couldn't have cared less about it.

I think we relaxed a little, then. We'd made our plans. It does help, to make plans.

'Like something to eat or drink? Before bed?'

'Couldn't face it.' I shook my head, then glanced across to check her sofa, where I'd probably be spending the night. It looked lush and cosy enough, to lie awake and toss about on.

She caught my thought; there were never any flies on Hermione. She said, hesitantly, 'You can share my bed, if you like. Providing you don't get the wrong idea. It's just that . . . I don't think I want to lie alone in the dark, thinking . . .'

It was the most wonderful offer a woman ever made me. Drunk with relief, I said, 'We can always leave the bedside light on . . .'

'I can't sleep with the light on . . .'

'I doubt I'm going to sleep anyway.'

She nodded. Then said, 'Have another whisky. I'll try not to be too long . . .'

'Nice warm relaxing bath?' I asked, feeling a bit more human.

'No.' She got up. 'Prayers, actually.'

'D'you *pray*?' I was shattered. I hadn't ever known anybody who'd prayed. Except James, of course, and my grandmother, and that was a very long time ago.

She lifted her head and made an embarrassed little speech to the corner of the ceiling. 'I pray very seldom, and very badly. But I have known prayers answered. And when you've got something very big and very nasty and very mysterious against you, it's a comfort to have something very big and very nice and very mysterious on *your* side. Now go and pour yourself another whisky. And, as I said, *don't* get the wrong idea.'

'Lady, tonight, even a teenage nymphomaniac would be safe from me.'

She managed a very small smile.

'Y'know, Jeff, you're not a bad guy to be in a nasty spot with.'

It was a crazy night. I heard most of 'Nightride' on Radio Two. Three times in the dark she reached out and gripped my hand, hard enough to squeeze it off. In the end, sleep came, and I had nightmares, and wakened up sweating and yelling.

But they were quite different kinds of nightmares. No rape.

Inside the white ship, the tiny skeletons began to move.

'Pleasant to see you again so soon!' Mr Makepeace flung back his silver hair from his high, mottled forehead with a huge hand. His deep-set little eyes took in my weariness, and Hermione's, that was even showing through her expertly-applied make-up. He gave a little smile, but kept his thoughts to himself. Probably told himself you never knew what young people got up to these days . . .

Hermione consulted her notes. 'We have dug up a large model steam-yacht called the *Circe*.' She was so calm, she might have been reading the nine o'clock news.

'The *Circe*,' said Mr Makepeace. 'Oh yes, I remember the *Circe*. How my poor father hated her! It spoilt our family breakfasts for all of three months.' He made a strange wheezing sound, that I thought might be laughing, and lit another cigarette from the tip of his last. It was such a poverty-stricken thing to do. And he obviously wasn't strapped for cash . . . I told myself I mustn't let my mind wander.

'What was the matter with her?' asked Hermione innocently, so innocently.

The old man frowned. 'She was too *big*. Vulgar. But then the Neptunes were always trying to outdo each other. I believe it took three people to get her into the water. And we had to make new jigs and buy new machine tools. Four feet in length was our usual limit, and that was stretching it. It cost that fool a fortune.

But he didn't care. He never cared about mere money. Threw it around like water. As I said, vulgar, vulgar.'

'What fool?' asked Hermione.

'J. Montague Wheeler,' said Mr Makepeace heavily. 'Ever hear a name like it? J. Montague Wheeler, with his silly great cigars. My father said he could hardly get his mouth round them. Everything had to be the biggest, for J. Montague Wheeler. That damned boat cost him nearly two thousand pounds, back in 1913. When a man could bring up a family on two guineas a week! He could have had another Rolls-Royce for the money. We had to make each part from scratch – couldn't use any of our standard parts at all.'

'Why was that?'

'Every damned thing had to work. Steering-wheel actually turned the rudder. Engine-room telegraphs actually responded in the engine-room. That took some doing, I can tell you, with sixteenth-of-an-inch brass rods! My father said it was almost as if the damned fool wanted to make himself tiny, like Alice in Wonderland, and sail the damned thing himself!'

I actually broke out in a cold sweat at that point, while the old man made his queer wheezing laugh. But Hermione didn't turn a hair, only coughed politely into her hand.

'He must have been very rich,' she said.

'Rich as Croesus. And didn't he let you know it! No breeding, no breeding at all. Oh, my poor father. He said he wouldn't make another, for all the tea in China. And then, to crown it all, we didn't get paid for the work. For seven years.'

'How was that?' asked Hermione. And even her

voice trembled. With fear? Or with the excitement of the chase? Strange girl, Hermione. Nice, but strange.

'Damned fellow vanished. Clean as a whistle. Took his family with him, too. Done a flit, my poor father said. Bankrupt. Nearly tore his hair out by the roots. But, you know, he mustn't have taken all his money with him. Because we *were* paid, seven years later, in 1920. Too late to do my poor father any good of course. Dead, serving his country. Killed at the Battle of Jutland, aboard HMS *Cheshire*. My eldest brother was running the firm by then. But we never made another as big as *Circe*. Is she for sale?'

'We don't know yet,' said Hermione. 'But if she is you'll have first refusal.'

The old man rumbled his approval. 'Any other way I can assist you, my dear?'

'Could you tell me any more about this J. Montague Wheeler?'

'M'father said he had the manners of a money-lender. East End money-lender. Very sharp about the pennies, for all his big spending. Went over the bills with a fine-tooth comb. We had to account for every penny. Of course, you've seen his photograph? With the rest of the "Neptune" lot? Showed you the other day . . .'

'Would you mind if we saw it again?'

The old boy bent to a low drawer in his desk, grunting so much I was afraid he might have a heart attack. Then the same mounting-card was passed across the desk; the same kerb of the Wheatstone Pond, the same trestles, and boats, the same row of pudgy sepia Edwardian faces, solemn behind big moustaches.

Well, not all the same, actually. J. Montague Wheeler was the same in general appearance, but there was one difference. Apart from dark eyes set too close together, which gave him a foxy look, and a too-long, fleshy nose, J. Montague Wheeler seemed to know a secret, and was gloating over it even in the face of the photographer. He had that little irritating kind of smile that makes you want to bash the owner's face in, after a bit. It was as if something intending no good was creeping up behind those good pompous self-made men, to do them down. And only J. Montague Wheeler knew about it, and rejoiced. His expression undercut the whole solemn picture. The longer you looked at it, the more it *dominated* the whole picture. Why had no one ever noticed it before? Why hadn't his friends noticed it at the time? If they *were* his friends . . .

'Looks a nasty piece of work, doesn't he?' said old Makepeace.

'He's . . . the only one with *two* sons?' asked Hermione. 'He has a hand on two boys' shoulders.'

'I don't know m'dear,' said old Makepeace regretfully.

'Do you think we might borrow this photograph, Mr Makepeace? For use in our exhibition?'

He frowned, mountainously. He was obviously charmed by her. But, equally obviously, he didn't like to part with any of his treasures. Then his brow cleared. 'Perhaps my no-good son could help you. He's got all kinds of gadgets in that drawing-office of his. He can make pictures very small, or even enlarge them if you like. Print them in full colour. Send them down the telephone to South America, if you believe all the nonsense he talks. We'll do you a nice enlargement. That do? Simon? *Simon*!' He raised his voice in an ancient bellow. His son appeared at the door, nervous as an office-boy. 'Simon, run down to the drawing-office and get the young lady a print of this. Enlarged. Much enlarged, eh?'

'Would you mind very much if I sent Miss Prentice? I happen to be on the phone to America . . .'

I will draw a veil over family quarrels that don't concern me. Suffice to say, we got our enlargement, and a very clear enlargement it was.

CHAPTER TEN

We sat in the front of Hermione's Metro, in the nearest lay-by, and stared at our enlargement. J. Montague Wheeler looked even nastier, enlarged. Every tiny line of his face was visible; they were great men, those old Edwardian photographers; beat the modern boys for detail every time. The impression that the awful man knew some Great Joke that nobody else knew grew stronger all the time.

And the two boys . . . one about fourteen, one a bit younger. That same look was on their faces too. It boded no good for the other Neptunes; come to that, it boded no good for the whole universe. It slowly made their faces into the faces of . . . certain photographs of the Kray twins, when they were in a relaxed mood . . . certain Nazi faces, wreathed in enjoyment over a game with an Alsatian dog. Faces that had stepped outside life, had seen life's stage scenery from the back, and knew what a fraud it was.

'Three of them,' said Hermione. 'And three skeletons in the boat . . . it's a big coincidence.'

'I doubt it,' I said, with a dry throat. 'They don't look like victims to me. They look more like the ones who did it. And sat back and laughed. They looked as if drowning baby monkeys would be very amusing, as far as they were concerned.'

We stared at the enlargement for another long time, and I for one was feeling worse and worse.

Finally, Hermione said, 'We can't sit here all day,' and rolled up the enlargement and put it back in its tube. 'We need to know *more*.'

'How?' My voice came out in a sort of wail.

'If somebody *this* rich vanished, it'd be in the papers. At the time. What we need is the local Wheatstone papers for 1913 . . . Wheatstone Public Library's what we need next.'

She started the car, and drove off, fast.

Wheatstone Public Library, in the afternoon, was a good place to lay ghosts. Unlike the rest of Gothic Wheatstone, almost in defiance of Gothic Wheatstone, it was a simple classical building in red brick and sandstone, like a well-mannered barn.

And the reference library was the least ghostly of all. Durable wall-to-wall carpeting, a neat beech reception-desk where middle-aged ladies requested books on the history of canals around London, the development of the English apple tree, or a reasoned catalogue of the products of the Bow Potteries in the eighteenth century. A fat good-natured bespectacled man took eager schoolchildren with spiral-backed notebooks through the development of the London Sewage System, or the imports of tanned hides through the East India Docks. Not so much educating them as telling them what to write in their projects. The air was loud with demands for rubbers, spare Biros, and the tinkle of dropped drawing-board clips.

And along one wall, the row of microfiche

machines, which we had to queue for, so great was the demand of housewives doing their family history.

We got machines in the end, and were now busy suffering. The chairs were half-broken rejects from the rest of the library, the machines were so well-used that the spools of microfiche film often came out of their clips. The turning-handles ran backwards if you let go of them, and often came off in your hand altogether, if you whirled them too vigorously. And there is something infinitely backache-creating in using a microfiche. Inside, things rattled; the print on the smoky golden screen kept going blurred; it was satisfactory neither to sit back wearing my reading-spectacles, nor to lean forward without them.

I was working through the copies of the long defunct weekly newspaper called the *Wheatstone Guardian*, while Hermione next door waded through the desert of the equally defunct *Wheatstone Advertiser*.

Big impressive newspapers, which did not confine themselves to the local news. They thought nothing of spending two columns on the doings of Lloyd George (with regard to the welfare of the citizens of Wheatstone). There were fascinating insights into the middle-aged Winston Churchill, ladies' fashions for the coming season, a cholera scare in the East End and Dr Collis Browne's Chlorodyne, recommended by all Army doctors to cure everything from enteric fever to whooping cough, by the look of it.

The only comfort was the touch of Hermione's knee on mine, as she sighed and whizzed through three more pages of foreign news and hat-adverts. It was hot and I kept dozing off. I was just turning the handle now, knowing that if anyone found anything, it would be her.

But her sudden hiss of breath made me come leaping awake, with a thudding heart.

'*Got* him,' she said. I looked across, and saw, small and dim as a postage stamp on her screen, the same pudgy face, the same smirk of a hidden joke. The small headline said:

MYSTERIOUS DISAPPEARANCE OF WHEATSTONE FAMILY

The print was too small and blurred for me to read more. So I just listened as she muttered to herself, and scribbled stuff into her notebook.

'Aged forty-two at the time of his disappearance. Well-known member of the Neptune Yacht Club. Was in business as an importer . . . oh, an address. Abbeywalk, Belvoir Road, Wheatstone.'

The room whirled around me. I remembered Abbeywalk: the queerness of the place; the heap of abandoned suitcases in the outhouse. But in particular I remembered the last entry in Annette le Feuvre's poor little diary:

They shall have me, but they shall not have him.

I had thought the 'they' had been her parents.

Now all I could think about was the three smirking, sneering faces in the picture of the Neptune Yacht Club (Steam Section).

The room went on whirling round me. The odd, mad behaviour, one Guy Fawkes' night, of Tony Tanner; just before he disappeared, leaving his precious model boats behind . . .

Where had all those people *gone*? And the suicides in the Pond? And that crazy fight between the firemen?

There was not just an ancient dreadful evil lingering on in Wheatstone . . . It was still working *now*.

'There's something wrong with that house,' I think I said. Then I was falling into darkness; the corner of the microfiche machine, the edge of the desk were cold and sharp. But they were the last things I knew.

She had left me lying very comfortably, on the *chaise-longue* pulled up to her sitting-room window; where the late afternoon sun would lie warm on the tartan rug over my legs, and the reassuring sounds of Kensington, women talking to dogs and men washing down cars, could drift in through the open window. There was whisky to hand; and a flask of coffee; and the latest editions of *Harper's* and *Cosmo*. There was even a cordless telephone. Oh, she had looked after me well. Before she went back to the chase.

I only hoped she'd get home before dark. For her sake and mine.

I dozed a lot, never quite unaware of the sun's warmth on my face, and the sounds outside; taking care never to drop into the dark depths where faces swam out of the darkness suddenly. It was pleasant just to drift and forget . . .

I'd had one fright: a rattle in the kitchen that had fetched me heart-thuddingly awake. But it was only her cat coming home through the cat-flap, the golden long-haired Suki, slender and elegant as Hermione herself, who had watched me first with caution, then with curiosity, and then come and decisively settled into my lap and gone to sleep.

133

Cats were wise; cats *knew*. While Suki slept on me relaxed, no harm could come to me . . .

The cordless phone rang, like a mewling lost mouse. I snatched it up, fumbled with the unfamiliar switches, and managed to remember her number.

'That you, guv?' The voice, warm and reassuring, of Sam. 'You OK? You sound a bit funny!' There was almost a smile in Sam's voice; probably at the idea of me shacked up in Hermione's house. He was much younger than James; his mind was broader. He was of the new generation who didn't bother to get married. 'We done OK, guv. We've been where you said. Dudley; Stafford. Got a good set of chairs for four hundred. Should get six for them, by the time they're polished up. And . . .' he took a deep breath, 'you ought to've seen the Welsh dresser at Martin's. Young fool had tarted it up wi' repro brass handles – thought it was Victorian. James rescued the old handles out of the bins in the yard. We knocked him down to two thou. James reckons it'll be worth five and a half. Late Georgian.'

'Well done,' I said. 'Where *is* James, by the way? Getting drunk to celebrate?'

Sam gave his infectious little giggle. James, like most Methodists, was a teetotaller. 'Knocked off early to see some of his holy mates in Birmingham. Bigwigs, I gather. Got something on his mind, James has.'

I cursed James in my mind. I knew what he had gone to talk to his holy mates about. And that after I'd sworn him to secrecy.

Much later, the mewling of the phone wakened me again. The look of the sky, a dimming blue with swallows wheeling, told me how late it was getting, and a tiny paw of panic nudged my stomach. But Hermione was in a high good mood, wild with excitement.

'Ran Wheeler down to earth, in an old copy of "Strange Stories from the *London Evening News*". The reference librarian put me on to it. He's a bit into the occult, and seems to have his own little book-cupboard, for those he favours. And, of course, this being a Wheatstone story, he knew all about it . . .

'Wheeler was an East Ender, and a no-good. A rag-and-bone man, no less, and had several convictions for helping himself to stuff left lying about. Used to work the Wheatstone District, back around nineteen hundred and seven or eight.

'Anyway, Abbeywalk wasn't built then. There was just a bit of derelict ground, with grand new houses growing up all round it, and a few tumble-down sheds among the undergrowth. Apparently he rented the sheds to run his rag-and-bone business from. Caused a hell of a stink among the *nouveaux riche* around there, but there wasn't much they could do about it.

'And then, and here's the crazy thing, suddenly he has lots of money to spend. Enough to buy the land he had been renting, and then he suddenly begins to build the present house, about 1911.

'People apparently hated the new house almost as much as they hated him; but again, in those free enterprise days, there was nothing they could do.

'Then he starts flinging his money about, trying to get himself popular, trying to buy his way into their society. There was no Mrs Wheeler: said he was a widower; but he flung himself into the social whirl all right. Garden fêtes for charity; wonderful displays of fireworks on Guy Fawkes' Night; inviting people to dinner. But he didn't get very far, wasn't liked. And complaints of strange noises coming from the house late at night, with lights on in the windows until 5 a.m., and the sound of orchestras playing, and yet no one seen coming or going. And a fuss about one or two children vanishing and never being seen again. Nobody important of course . . . little serving-girls, boot-boys whose parents were too poor and crushed to make much fuss.

'And then he joined the Neptune Yacht Club. Damned fool secretary let him join because he lived out of the district himself, and didn't know what Wheeler was like. Apparently it was very grand, the Neptune in those days. Wheeler tried to win the yacht-sailing races, but was almost too fat to handle the boats he bought; so he failed. Much laughter. Then he turned his hand to steam-yachts. Won the *concours d'élégance*, in 1912, by sheer weight of money, and Ross and Makepeace skill . . .

'There was another move to get rid of him, but it failed. And he vowed to come back the following year, and show such a thing as would not be believed. District all agog, in spite of themselves.

'And then, one night, he just vanished. With his two sons. Gave the staff – cook and housemaids – an extra evening off and they came in late and tiptoed up to bed so as not to disturb the family. The following morning, the housemaid takes in the early morning tea – no one there, the beds not slept in. After a day going hairless, they brought in the police.

'No signs of forced entry, no signs of violence.

Only one thing missing – the lovely new model steam-yacht they'd spent the previous three days fiddling with, ever since it came from Ross and Makepeace. It had its own little four-wheeled cart for conveying it about, and that was found by the shore of the Pond.

'The Police dragged the Pond of course, for three days, but nothing unusual turned up. They thought the family had done a flit, and contacted Wheeler's solicitor, who was as puzzled as they were. The one thing he knew was that Wheeler had made most of his money speculating on the stock exchange. They waited for the usual things then – creditors to turn up, withdrawals from the bank – nothing. Wheeler didn't owe anybody anything, apart from Ross and Makepeace. He never tried to draw his money out, and there was close to £30,000 in the bank – that's about three million by today's standards.

'After that – not a sign of them from that day to this. After seven years, the solicitor had them presumed dead, by the court, and that's when Ross and Makepeace must've finally been paid.'

'Was there any will?' I managed to get out at last.

'No will – no known relatives, though one or two people tried it on in the East End, and one man went to prison for attempted fraud. All the money went to the government in the end, under the intestacy laws. What do you make of that?'

'Phew,' I said feebly. 'Are you coming home now?'

'No, I've managed to contact a reporter on the current local paper. We're going for a drink in about quarter of an hour. He wants to write up our dig, but I'm going to pick his brains about Abbeywalk . . .'

'You will come straight home after that?' I asked anxiously.

'I suppose so . . .' She sounded reluctant, still high on the thrills of the chase. 'Why – are you all right, Morgan?' There was a tinge of contempt in her voice, that stung.

'I'll manage – till then.' I was aware of the sky outside growing dimmer still. The swallows had gone to their nests. 'Take care, Hermione.'

'Oh, don't worry about me. I'm used to handling reporters.'

She rang off.

But it wasn't reporters I was worried about.

Soon after dark, the phone went again. I'd been off the couch once, to go to the loo, and make myself a sandwich I didn't want, and put all the lights on and drawn the curtains. I felt so weary, so helpless. Things were happening to me; I wasn't happening to anything.

It wasn't her; it was James.

'Mr Morgan, I want a word.' James at his most formidable; the other side of him, Holy James. As usual I wondered what had happened to the cheerful rogue who could swap the white painted dial of a long-case clock for a repro brass-face, sell the thing for twice the money and not turn a hair . . . nobody like James for being two separate halves.

'I've put our case to some friends of mine who know about such things. Who've spent years studying them . . .'

'What case is this, James?' I said very coldly. Really, I was worried about Hermione, and what she was getting up to, out there in the dark.

'That steam-yacht . . .'

'I told you not to mention that to anybody, James. You *promised* . . .'

'There's some things too important for our human promises. The Lord . . . I went to Him in prayer and he told me to go and tell them . . .'

Oh, these impossible people who go to the Lord in prayer. Why does He always seem to tell them to do exactly what they want to do anyway?

'Very convenient . . .'

'Now don't be like that, Mr Morgan. I know you're an unbeliever, but we can't allow that to hinder the Lord's Work. *We* think that real evil is at work here. Not just human wickedness, but Evil Incarnate that must be trampled down before it spreads. They're prepared to . . .'

'Look, James, can't this wait? I'm expecting an urgent phone call . . .'

'Not as urgent as this, Mr Morgan. Our adversary the Devil goeth about as a roaring lion, seeking whom he may devour, whom resist steadfast in the faith. My friends have told me such things you wouldn't believe. Right here in Birmingham. The kind of stuff that never reaches the newspapers . . . this could . . . this *is* . . . a matter of life and death, Mr Morgan. More important than life and death . . .'

'You sound like Bill Shankly talking about football . . .'

'You can scoff, Mr Morgan. But I don't think you'll go on scoffing for much longer. Something could be happening this very night. I wouldn't want some other poor soul drowning themselves in the Wheatstone Pond . . .'

139

That touched a vital nerve. And in my pain and terror, I said something very rude about him and his religion.

There was a long and nasty silence, then he said, slowly, and keeping his temper with a great effort, 'I feel sorry for you, Mr Morgan.'

Then there was a click, and the dialling tone resumed, and in the silence that followed, it felt like I'd turned away my last friend.

And for what? For daring to say out loud what I'd only been thinking? Why do we modern people mince words in such a mealy-mouthed way? If there was not Evil Incarnate in that house, there was the next best thing to it, and no amount of clever, reasonable psychological jargon was going to make it go away. I saw again, vivid in my mind's eye, those tiny skeletons, and, in the face of them, clever reasonable psychological jargon was dumb.

I began to pace up and down, while Suki watched me with impassive curiosity. Why do we pace up and down, exhausting ourselves?

Before I had time to entirely exhaust myself, the phone rang again.

Oh, how good it was to hear her warm, living breathing voice.

'Morgan? There's some more stuff come out. D'you know, of those seven suicides in the Pond, over the last five years, four of them had bed-sitters at Abbeywalk? As Mike said, he knows it's bed-sitter land, and bed-sitter land is bad for suicides, but this is not just coincidence. The reporters know; they talk about it among themselves. That last little girl who used to come into your shop, Margie Duff, she had a bed-sitter there. She'd only been in it three weeks. The only tenant. But it was cheap; she couldn't afford anything better. Morgan, you still there?'

I was. But the world was reeling about me again. Little Margie Duff, with her hopeful little smile, who so wanted to be liked, approved of. What had happened to *her* in that house? It was unbearable to even contemplate . . .

'I'm still here,' I said.

'I'm just going up there to have a look around. I won't be long . . .'

'Don't! For God's sake, don't!'

'Steady, Morgan. Don't panic. I won't do anything stupid. I'll be home inside an hour. I'll fetch in a take-away . . .'

'You won't be able to get into that house. It's locked up solid. I've *tried* it.'

'Then no harm can come to me, can it? I just thought there might be a broken window in the basement . . .'

'Look, I can organize a way in for you. I'm sure Mossy can arrange it. We could do it properly, together. Tomorrow night, if you like . . .'

'I happen to feel like going up there tonight, Morgan. On my own. I'm a big girl now. *I've* been looking after *you* today, remember? So how come you think you can organize *my* life?' The phone rattled, and I heard her say, over her shoulder, 'All right, Mike. Just another half, then. I have to be getting on . . .' Then she said, 'I'm going to have another drink with Mike. I'll be home by eleven. Take care. And you could feed Suki. It's long past her time. I wonder she hasn't been pestering you . . . See you.'

'Hermione!' I shouted. 'They have a Homewatch Scheme up Belvoir Road. They're very twitchy. If you get arrested for burglary, it won't do you much good with the City Toy Museum . . .'

Then I realized I was spinning my lies to the dialling tone.

CHAPTER ELEVEN

I shall never understand myself. I am so many different people. One minute I was a scared timid doormat, and the next I was moving like a whirlwind. Shoes on, raincoat on. By the phone in her kitchen, a card for a minicab firm was pinned up. And, miraculously, they answered straight away.

'I want a cab to Wheatstone – fast. And I'm willing to pay for speed.'

There was a hint of a smile in the man's voice. 'Got just the man for you, squire. He'll be with you in two minutes.'

I rummaged frantically until I found her big torch; shoved a small bottle of brandy in my pocket and picked a big heavy walking-stick, with a knob of brass for a head, from the umbrella rack by her front door. That stick was deceptive; like so many things Victorian it had thoughtful hidden depths. Reverse it in your hand, hold the bottom ferrule, and it becomes a club that will easily cave in anybody's skull. Victorian foot-pads didn't have it all their own way . . .

A middle-sized car turned in at the mews, and went past me like a rocket. I chased after it wildly, as it did a tight three-point turn; it nearly knocked me down twice; then I fell through the held-open door, and squirmed to arrange myself in the narrow but deep bucket seat. As I groped for a safety-belt, the acceleration hit me like a fist.

'Where to in Wheatstone, squire?'

'Belvoir Road; know it?'

'You show me, eh?'

It must have been about ten. The wide tree-lined roads of inner London were amazingly empty under the high yellow neons. Everyone who was driving anywhere had got there, and it was not yet time for them to set out back home. The car cornered in a way that left my stomach skidding sideways.

He seemed to be doing about ninety down the straights.

'Golf GTI is it?' I asked, to show I wasn't terrified.

'Nah. Lancia Delta 4×4. There's only about four hundred of them in this country. Me insurance is £1400 a year . . .'

I glanced at him sideways. He was very small and very trim; the kind of trimness that PE instructors had, when I did my National Service. Big pectorals under a grubby ELF T-shirt. Jeans, trainers. Short dark curly hair, and three days growth that was not designer-stubble.

He cut across a number 13 Hammersmith bus at the lights, with less than a foot to spare. 'I only do this to pay for this bugger,' he said. 'She's worse than a wife. Eats me out of house and home . . .'

I reached into my wallet and tossed two tens on to the dashboard. They immediately fell off, on to the floor, among a heap of oily rags. But he nodded and gave a grunt of satisfaction. I felt he was a good bloke to have on my side.

'Ever have bother with the police?'

He grinned, a far-away remembering grin. 'No contest. They're underpowered. Suspensions as soft as shit. Policemen can't drive . . .'

Should tyres be making that screeching noise?

'We're in Wheatstone, squire,' he said warningly, after a bit. My startled wits saw my own shop flashing past. I managed to stammer out, 'Straight on past the Park gates. Then first left . . .'

It was a leap, from a world of physical terror, to one of mental terror. 'Fourth on the right,' I said. 'Would you mind parking in the drive? With your headlights full on?'

He grunted, discouragingly. I said, 'I'll pay you for your waiting time.'

He grunted again, contentedly. We screeched to a stop, and he flicked on full beam.

He had quartz-halogens, of course. They made the whole crazy front, with its glass canopy like a helmet, seem to burn with orange fire. Behind the house, the outhouse where the suitcases lay was outlined like a solitary flame.

I got out stiffly, and hefted my stick. Left to himself, he flicked the courtesy light on, and settled to a book on car maintenance.

I walked up to the front door and tried it. What a relief to find it locked hard. I gave it a couple of kicks, to make sure; more out of spite, really. The echoes faded away inside. It sounded like the hall floor and staircase were bare boards.

Encouraged, I walked around and tried the back door. It was softly illuminated by the headlights reflecting off the outhouse. Locked hard. I kicked twice again; ran my torch over the windows, downstairs, upstairs. No broken glass.

No more doors. No broken windows. There were steps down to a cellar. No open windows there, either;

though some kind of monstrous white growth of fungus was oozing out of the brickwork. I was very glad there was no point to venturing down those steps . . .

So, we'd beaten her to it. She'd still be finishing her last drink with Mike. She couldn't possibly be inside . . . Could she? So why was I imagining her, tiptoeing up those dark stairs? Suppose the front door had swung shut behind her? She'd be trapped . . .

Irrationally, I turned to the front door, to try it again.

It swung open, under my hand, as I tried the handle . . .

All the confidence I'd built up over the last half-hour just collapsed. I only had enough left to push the front door open, shine the torch in, get a glimpse of a wide bare stair leading up into darkness, with a cardboard box, poised to fall, about half-way up. Then the door swung shut on me again. I swear there was malice in that door. It would always swing shut; it might lock behind you . . . somehow I *knew* it was a trap.

I gave it another shove, full of spiteful force, so it banged back against the wall. I yelled in, 'Hermione? Hermione?'

The house diminished my voice to an echoing squeak. But I felt I had done something foolish; somehow, hearing those echoes, I became convinced she was in there. And somehow, part of myself was now in there with her.

I looked round for something to prop the door open with. But there was nothing handy . . .

Except that cardboard box, half-way up the stairs. If

I pushed the door a third time, and made a run for it, I could be back with that box before the door swung shut . . . I was sure I could.

I took a deep breath . . .

And then I heard two brief toots on the car's horn. I spun round, and saw there was someone in a long white raincoat talking to the driver.

Hermione had a white raincoat . . .

I ran back.

It *was* Hermione, furious with me. 'What the blazes are you doing, Morgan? You've got the place lit up like the Fourth of July. This your idea of a secret reconnaissance? I wonder you didn't lay on a red carpet and the Brigade of Guards Band . . .'

'Look,' I said. 'It's not the right time. That house is . . .'

'Bedamned to the right time. I've come for a look, and I'm going to have a look.' She pushed me aside, and made for the front door. It swung open, under her hand.

'Don't go in there!' I yelled, grabbing her by the arm.

'Leave go of me. Who do you think you are?'

We were wrestling now. She was punching at me, and it hurt. She was yelling her head off. I couldn't hold her much longer.

And then we heard the police siren. We stopped, oddly in each other's arms, listening.

The police siren was getting nearer. Much nearer.

It died, as the panda swept in at the gate and skidded on the gravel behind my minicab. Two car doors slammed, one just after the other. Footsteps on the gravel.

'What seems to be the trouble, sir?'

We fell into stammering embarrassed farce. We both said different things, and I don't think the young constable could make head nor tail of any of it. We collapsed into silence.

In which I heard the other officer talking to my minicab driver.

'Lovers's tiff, I reckon,' said the minicab driver. And, at that same moment, I felt a patch of wetness spreading down the outside of my thigh. I groped for it, and smelt my fingers. Brandy. Our struggles must have loosened the screw-top. As the heat of my body warmed it, I began to smell like a distillery. I saw the young constable's nostrils work gently.

'Are you in charge of a motor vehicle, sir?'

'No,' I said exasperatedly. 'I came by that minicab.'

'Very wise, sir. And have you been drinking, madam?'

'I've had a couple,' said Hermione. 'But I'm not drunk.'

'Would you accompany me to the patrol car, madam? I shall require you to . . .'

As I said, screaming farce. Except that before he led her humbly away, he leaned between us and tried that front door for himself.

It wouldn't budge. He twisted the handle this way and that, put his shoulder against it, even kicked it. To no effect whatever. I *knew* then I'd missed a trap, by the skin of my teeth.

'According to our records, sir, this house has been empty for some time . . .' There was a question in his voice.

'I was calling on a girl I used to know . . .' It seemed the wisest thing to say.

'Her name, sir?'

Without thinking, I said, 'Margie Duff.'

He sighed, and relaxed. 'I'm afraid she no longer lives here, sir. She died.' I walked with him to the patrol car, while he tactfully broke the news I already knew. They're pretty good, some of these young policemen; very compassionate; it must be the new training . . .

We found that Hermione had missed losing her licence by about a millimetre. The constable gave her a stern lecture on the evils of drinking and driving.

Which she nagged me about, all the way to her place.

CHAPTER TWELVE

Mossy gently parked the car under some trees at the top end of Belvoir Road, eased the hand-brake on and consulted his watch.

'Right,' he said, 'just on ten. They'll all be settled into the big movie or the ten o'clock news. Nobody on the way out to make a cup o' cocoa yet. 'Less we're unlucky. Right, I'll just go over it again. I'll drop you down the road, two hundred yards apart. Walk nice and slow, as if you're just out for a stroll. Don't catch the one in front up, whatever you do. Go in the gate one by one – it's less conspicious.

'I'll drop our Dickie here last – he'll be in front, carrying the briefcase. He'll pick the back-door lock, wedge the door with the briefcase so it don't slam shut on you, give you a quick double-whistle, and go on to the outhouse. Now, in the outhouse, Dickie, go through them suitcases. It's only *papers* out of them we want, right? Don't go light-fingered on me, right? And I'll stay in the car, by the front gate, and keep a good look-out. An' if I toot me horn three times sharp, you get out of there as fast as your little legs will carry you – down the garden and over the wall an' into the Park. You should be able to lose the fuzz among the trees, or if you can't, get together an' act the courting couple. Nothing puts the fuzz off like courting couples – the fuzz is a mass of sexual frustration brought on by working shifts an' too much over-time . . .'

Good old Mossy, I thought. Whatever happens, he's in the clear. Innocently sitting in a parked car is no crime . . . Still, it was good of him to oblige, particularly with Dickie, a thin cadaverous youth with the air of an apprentice bullfighter, till he opened his mouth and spoke a few words of broad Cockney.

'Right, then.' Mossy gently started the engine and rolled away down Belvoir Road, keeping the revs down to be as silent as possible. There was just the hiss of tyres on the wet lamplit road.

I dropped off first, feeling the touch of rain on the back of my neck. Looking ahead, I saw the car stop again for just a moment, and the white flash of Hermione's mack under a street-lamp. There was a strong impulse to hurry, to catch her up and ask point-lessly what was going on. Then I saw the flash of Mossy's brake-lights, as he parked. Somewhere in front, Dickie must be fiddling with the back-door lock of Abbeywalk.

I nipped in sharp through the gateway and under the trees; and bumped straight into Hermione. Before we'd got our breath back, there came Dickie's low whistle.

'Let's go arm-in-arm,' whispered Hermione. 'Prac-tise being a courting couple.' She giggled, but it was the giggle of nerves.

So we went, arm in arm, snuggling together against . . . what?

There was the open door, with the black briefcase jammed half-way through it, glinting in a stray ray of a distant street-lamp. Hermione slipped through. As I followed, my foot caught the briefcase and kicked it right across the floor. I snatched at the door behind me just in time. It was on the point of closing; it nipped my fingers painfully. As she went across to grope for the briefcase, her feet echoed hollowly on the floor-boards, and somehow I sensed cellars below.

'Upstairs first,' said Hermione. I followed her out of the scullery door, by the light of her torch. Through a large, empty kitchen, where a tap dripped like an off-beat clock, into a hall with filthy black-and-white tiles.

It was at this point that all fear left me. I felt a great surge of confidence. Almost as if I was among friends. C'mon, I tried to warn myself. Wise up. This is a dreadful house; people have died here, maybe been killed.

But it was no use. My confidence rose in great waves. I was invincible; I was the master of my soul; master of the universe. Of course, I should have grabbed Hermione and run then. But all I did was follow her.

I watched her climb the staircase, by the light of her torch and mine. I saw, so clearly, the beauty of her long, slender legs, the smoothness of the calf-muscles, moving as soft as cream under the black nylon stockings. From the dead-straight seams I knew she must be wearing stockings, and not tights. Somewhere, under the concealing folds of that raincoat, there must be opulent patches of white flesh. I began to want to see those patches, very much. And I could see no reason why I should not see those patches, very soon. What was there to stop me? We were alone . . .

On the landing, Hermione turned. She said, harshly, triumphantly, 'This will show the bastards!'

'Which bastards?' I said, without interest. Under

her open coat, I could see her skirt, and under her skirt, the luscious near-flatness of her belly. I should soon sample that, now, too.

'The bastards at the City Toy Museum. They've kept me in my place for long enough. Just because I'm young. And a woman. When we solve this, they'll *have* to notice me. I want the deputy-director's job. They'll have to sack him. He's away ill half the time. I'm not having him standing in my way.'

She turned to carry on up the stairs. Her raincoat swung back, displaying the small sharp points of her breasts. On, blind Hermione, you think you're going on to fame and glory. You don't know what you are walking into. Somewhere ahead, there will be a bed. Maybe an unmade bed, or just a bare urine-stained mattress. So much the better, proud, beautiful Hermione. I will roll you not in the luxury you are used to, but in the staleness of sweat and filth and dust and dead flies. Then you will realize the world is not about the City Toy Museum, and your own great glory . . . but she was running on.

'I can soon get rid of the Director, too. I know quite a lot of things about him, that our trustees don't know. Things he's sold at a profit, that he should have kept for the Museum. The affair he had with that little whore in the Dolls' Department. Oh, they won't give him time to clear his desk, once I tell them . . .'

How surprised you will be, Hermione, when I leap on you. The incredulity on your face, as I begin to tear your clothes . . . oh, you'll fight and claw. But I'm strong, strong. I shall enjoy it more if you fight. There will be more chance to hurt you . . .

'Of course, I shan't stay long, once they give me the Directorship. Just a couple of years, to make a name.

Then I shall go on to America. An exchange visit; meet some big American scholar who wants an affair ... they're a randy lot, always trying to touch you up, on the sly, at conferences ...'

All this time, she was opening doors and shining her torch into empty rooms. Rooms with dirty mattresses thrown askew, with torn half-posters on the walls and the bodies of long-dead rats in corners. Taking no more notice of them than I was.

Oh, Hermione, how I shall explore you! How I shall explore your fear, your pleadings, the delicious point when you at last give up hope.

We had reached the last attic.

'Nothing here,' she said, with little interest, automatically. 'Let's try the cellars ...'

I looked from her to the unmade bed ... but no, it would be better in the cellars; darker, filthier. Somewhere to bury the poor bloody rag of her body, when I was finally done with her.

So, in mock obedience, I began to follow her downstairs again. Could I, could I, when I had reduced her to a bloody rag of a woman, remake her, make her perfect and happy again, so I could tear her to bits all over again? As many times as I wished, till the world's end. How would her blood taste, on my fingers ...?

Somewhere, far away, as we reached the first floor landing again, came three toots of a car-horn. They meant nothing to me. It might have been some pointless lost night-bird calling.

'Men are pathetic,' she called back at me, from the bottom stair. 'Their brains are between their legs. Their whole being is between their legs ...'

Oh, no, Hermione, foolish Hermione, dead

Hermione, my brains are in my *fingers* too. That's right, my poor love, go to the cellar door, open it, descend . . .

Again came the three toots of a car-horn. More urgent now. What was there, in the world out there, to be urgent about? Poor pathetic piffling people . . .

At that moment, an alien figure of utter fury leapt on to me. Strong, invincible though I was, he was so much stronger . . . he almost picked me up bodily, and carried me to the back door. Threw me down the back steps, shouting meaningless gibberish.

'Run, you silly effer, run!'

I landed painfully on my knees. Suddenly, I was Morgan again: little, hurting, and quite terrified of being caught by the police. I leapt to my feet, stared around me wildly.

The flying figure in a white raincoat cannoned into me and we both fell down again. A dark figure with a briefcase in its hand took off like a rocket down the wilderness of the back garden. Dickie, as if all the devils in hell were after him.

'Run, Morgan, run.' It was Hermione's ordinary voice; she sounded as terrified of being caught by the police as I was. We got up and blundered down the dark obstacles of the garden. I held my hands as a stirrup for her foot, and almost threw her over the garden wall. Then we were running for the cover of the Park trees . . .

'I would have thought, Mr Morgan,' said Sergeant Crittenden heavily, 'that if you two had wanted to go in for that kind of thing, you would have found somewhere more comfortable. Your place, sir? Or her place, here? Seems a very nice little hideaway for a spot of fornication between consenting adults.'

He glanced around Hermione's living-room with interest.

They had let us go from the police station an hour ago. But here was Crittenden, bright as a bird. Obviously his turn for the night shift, this week.

'It's the lure of the open air, on a lovely night,' said Hermione coolly. 'And, I suppose, the risk of being caught. A feeling of illicitness gives an edge, sergeant. Guy de Maupassant wrote a short story on the topic, once . . .'

'I am very well aware, madam, that de Maupassant wrote a short story on the topic. I read it, in the French original, when I was in the sixth form.'

In other words, don't come the culture vulture with me, madam. He went on, 'You hadn't . . . been doing further investigations, madam?'

'At the Pond, sergeant? No, not after dark. I'm not that keen.'

'I didn't mean at the Pond, madam. I meant at the premises known as Abbeywalk in Belvoir Road . . .'

'I'm not quite sure where that is, sergeant.' Oh, what a lovely cool distant liar the girl was.

'I find that strange, madam. Considering I have a report of a lady and gentleman having a row on the doorstep of Abbeywalk, the previous evening. The lady, apparently, was all for gaining admittance, the gentleman was violently trying to dissuade her. Their descriptions, well, it might have been you and Mr Morgan, madam. Though the gentleman reeked of brandy, which is *not* like Mr Morgan.'

'Nothing to say about that, sergeant. Except that having a row on a doorstep is not a crime,' she said.

'We seem to have had a run of non-crimes round Abbeywalk, recently. One Mossy Hughes, sitting in a parked car outside the premises. We got him for sounding his horn after dark, and while stationary . . . he should get all of a twenty-pound fine for that, with his record. And another gentleman, name of Dickie Warren, found leaving Wheatstone Park with a brief-case full of ancient correspondence that did not belong to him. Does that ring any kind of bell, madam?'

Hermione had the grace to drop her head.

'I should take this all very seriously, except that Abbeywalk, on examination, proved to be securely locked up, with no sign of an entry having been forced. And the fact that there is not one thing in Abbeywalk worth even a junk-merchant stealing.'

'You seem very interested in Abbeywalk, sergeant? Considering. Hardly seems worth police time.' I felt I had to keep my end up, even if I did feel like death. But it was so unreal, this piddling talk of petty crime, when an hour ago I might have been standing with my hands thick with Hermione's blood . . .

'It may *interest* you to know, Mr Morgan, that we have been through the contents of Mr Dickie Warren's briefcase, for which he cannot account. We found letters addressed to ten people, at the Abbeywalk address. Seven of them are on the National Police Computer as missing persons . . .'

We were both silent. We could find nothing to say. A dread was coming over me again. Dreads had been coming over me ever since the two constables caught us.

'Abbeywalk smells *nasty* to me, Mr Morgan. The nastiest thing I've smelt since I was on the Dennis Nilsen case. Remember the Nilsen case, Mr Morgan? Young boys murdered and cut up and flushed down the toilet? Well, that's how Abbeywalk *smells*. And that's before you include those suicides in the Pond. Of people who lived there . . .'

Again, we were silent. He got up to go; said, standing in the doorway, 'If there's one thing I hate more than criminals, it's the members of the public who won't help. Because it's not convenient. It's people like you who pay me to be a policeman, and do your dirty work for you. And then you hamper me in doing it. Seems like you're wasting your own hard-earned money . . .'

He said it with such disgust.

'Would you like a supper-drink, before we go to bed?' asked Hermione. Her face was deathly; there were big shadows under her eyes. Then she said, 'Hell, I don't *want* to go to bed. I don't dare shut my eyes. Tonight, in that house, I was planning to do all kinds of horrible things . . . that weren't me at all.'

'I know,' I said. 'You told me about them. At the City Toy Museum.'

'I was v.ishing people ill – iller. I was wishing people *dead*.'

'I know. And I was planning to rape and murder you. And bring you back to life so I could rape and murder you all over again.' Without warning, I began retching, and finally was sick on her best rug. I must say she was very kind; she didn't nag; she held my head and wiped me down afterwards. I felt very cold and shivery, and she put the gas fire on.

'What *was* it, Morgan? Are we both going mad?'

'We're sane enough now,' I said bitterly. 'I'd be sane enough now, even if I'd murdered you. And I was just waiting to do it. Once you were down the cellar. If Mossy hadn't tooted his horn, if Dickie hadn't hauled us out, you'd be dead now . . .'

'I didn't reckon you for that kind of man . . .'

'As the feminists say: all men are rapists . . .' I had this need to grovel, to sick it up, to cleanse myself. My father always said confession was good for the soul.

'I knew you fancied me. But . . . rape? Murder? *Really?*'

'I wanted to lay you – take you down a peg.'

'That's hardly *murder*, Morgan!'

'No,' I said wretchedly.

'I'd had some nasty thoughts about people at the Museum. But I'd never have done anything about it. Not in a month of Sundays.'

'I suppose that's what keeps us on the rails. Timidity. Respectability. Fear of consequences. But somehow, tonight, I didn't feel there would be any consequences. I felt invincible. Full of power. It seems so . . . pathetic, now.'

'That's how J. Montague Wheeler must have felt. Full of power.'

'A rag-and-bone man, who suddenly made a lot of money . . . What's *inside* that house, Hermione?'

'I don't know. But it's down in the cellar. I could *feel* it.'

'Offering unlimited power? To do evil?'

'The name . . . Abbeywalk. Was there ever an abbey round here. A medieval abbey? Or is the name just a romantic fantasy?'

159

'Oh, there was a medieval Abbey of Wheatstone. Its coat of arms is still the coat of arms of the Borough. They boast about it in their handbook. All gone now. Except some reckon the Wheatstone Pond was their fish-ponds . . .'

'Suppose the monks . . . no, that's just silly.'

'Go on. It's all ridiculous anyway, in this day and age.'

'Suppose the monks . . . were exorcists? Medieval priests practised exorcism. Suppose they were called upon to deal with something dreadful. And they couldn't destroy it or cast it out. Suppose all they could do was bring it back with them and keep it under lock and key, safe . . . with a binding prayer or spell or something. Maybe they kept it alive to investigate it, muck about with it. Then, when the Abbey was dissolved by Henry the Eighth, they had to go, and leave it behind.

'Nobody came; nobody built on the site. Houses go up all round in the nineteenth century, but nobody wants to build on the actual site. And then this rag-and-bone man comes along, mooching around for things to steal . . . and he rents the waste land . . . with a few old buildings on it . . . and quite soon he has all the money in the world . . . to buy the land and build the house. And then he vanishes. But *it* remains behind in the house. And people come to live there. And people vanish . . .'

I said stupidly, like you always do, 'For God's sake, Hermione, this is the twentieth century.'

'Maybe we've found a gap in the twentieth century. A black hole that people fall into. And there's no reason in the world why people shouldn't go on falling into it. Poor people who don't have anybody who cares about them . . . people at the end of their tether. There's always somebody wanting a cheap bed-sitter . . .'

'Stop it. I want to sleep tonight. This is pure speculation!'

'That thing nearly killed me tonight, Morgan. And what would it have done to you? Don't you want to know what nearly destroyed you? What destroyed Tony Tanner and Margie Duff?

'And the Wheatstone Pond, Morgan! It's downhill from that house. Stuff must be draining down into it, all the time. Stuff that set those two firemen fighting each other, that turned my students so stroppy. Stuff that the pumps are still pumping into the drainage system . . .'

'Stuff from *what*? This is crazy!'

'It fits all the facts, doesn't it?'

The trouble was, I couldn't find fault with her argument. It was a crude working hypothesis. All the facts did fit. For the moment.

In its own way, it was a kind of dreadful relief. We knew the worst now; or the worst our minds could visualize. All the other facts in our mind, from years gone by, moved over and jiggled about to make room for it. It fell into place; it *was*.

And with that fitting-in came a humble, dreadful weariness. I knew we should go to sleep when we went to bed. We would sleep in a world where the thing existed. We would wake up to a world where it existed . . .

'Tomorrow,' said Hermione, 'we go and see the house agent.'

*

The house agent had his office in a quite different part of London. A palatial place, with an all-glass front. Built during the boom, maybe. Now, in the slump, his windows were still full of houses for sale; but several desks behind were empty, with idle phones and dust-covers over the word processors.

No doubt if there hadn't been a slump in the housing market, he wouldn't have had time to see us. But you could tell he hadn't been doing anything. The chrome balls of his executive toy were still moving, infinitesimally.

A tall, well-built man in his forties; blond hair bleached by the sun, very tanned. Not a tan acquired in England.

There were several bits of golfing memorabilia on his desk. Maybe he took golfing holidays in Mallorca. My heart sank. I never met a golfer yet with a big heart. Or a big brain. Still, he fancied Hermione well enough to get to his feet and shake hands.

'Abbeywalk?' he said. 'An interesting property. In a sought-after district.'

'You've seen it?' asked Hermione.

'Only photographs. I don't keep dogs and bark myself.'

His small dark eyes priced us up and down. 'You don't give the *impression* of needing a cheap bed-sitter . . .'

'We're interested in buying the house,' said Hermione. 'Or could be.'

'On whose behalf?'

'I'm not empowered to say at the moment.'

'I hope they've got a big bank account.' He said it very offensively. 'In any case, it's not for sale. Not at any price. My client was absolutely adamant about that. Rent, yes, welcome. Sale, no. There is considerable development potential, when the market picks up again. Besides, my client has no need of the money. He passes most of the time travelling the world, spending it. I wish I had his loose change . . .'

'Who is your client?'

'I am not empowered to divulge his name. He has no wish to be bothered. He made that quite clear when he handed the house over to us, last year.'

'So some other agent had it before you?'

'Some other agent, yes. Again, I am not empowered to divulge the name . . .'

'Everyone seems very cagey. Have there been complaints?'

'Not that I know of.' But his blink-rate went up quite markedly. 'May I ask just who you *are* representing, madam?'

'I am not empowered to divulge his name,' snapped Hermione.

'Then I think I will wish you good day. Miss Hereford will show you out.' He pressed a buzzer on his desk.

Miss Hereford was a big girl; and there was an even bigger man standing behind her, craning his head to get a look at us.

There was nothing to do but go.

As we regained the street, Hermione said, 'That's all you need for a black hole to survive in our society. Somebody who couldn't care less. Providing he's paid well enough. I think he thought we were TV people. There *has* been trouble.'

I stared sadly at the passing buses and taxis. They

were trying to persuade me that life was OK and quite normal.

They weren't making a very good job of it.

'Do you think the present owner *knows*?' I said. 'He's getting all that money from *somewhere*. And I'll bet it's not by renting bed-sitters.'

CHAPTER THIRTEEN

We were still drinking our first coffee and smoking our first cigarettes next morning, in our dressing-gowns, when there came a heavy knocking at the door. A peremptory knocking, a knocking of authority that made the front door seem very thin.

'Fuzz?' asked Hermione wearily.

'Sergeant Crittenden rides again. I'll let him in.' I went down, fearing what he might have to tell us.

But it wasn't the fuzz. It was my employee, James. Except that he didn't look like my employee; he gave me a look of grand contempt and said, 'Mr Morgan, may we come in?' There were three others, gloomy large men in long dark overcoats in spite of the sunny morning. They looked like they never took them off. They made the police look like boy scouts in bob-a-job week.

They settled on to Hermione's graceful little chairs, and turned her cosy lounge into a court of law. Worse than a court of law.

Mr Maidment. Mr Crombie. Mr Shaftesbury. I fixed it in my mind that Mr Maidment was quite old, with a nearly entirely bald head when he finally took his dark trilby hat off. Just a few dark strands combed across, like seaweed on an empty beach. Mr Crombie was the youngest, not much over forty. Mr Shaftesbury was the one who was neither Mr Maidment nor Mr Crombie. They had not offered to shake hands. They put down their hats as if fearing pollution wherever they put them. They looked at the room, at the little untidinesses, and turned it into a brothel. They looked at Hermione and turned her into a tart. They looked at me and turned me into a fallen sinner.

Mr Maidment looked at me harder still.

'Tell us, Mr Morgan, what has happened since James left you?'

I tried asking myself who the hell he thought he was, but it was no use. Their authority, their certainty, their righteousness was a wall you could hammer against till your fists bled, and it wouldn't do any good. I had not felt so small since the last time my headmaster summoned me to his study, back in 1958.

So I began to tell them all that had happened. It seemed the easiest way to get rid of them. I was looking for paths of least resistance by that time. They were good listeners, I'll say that for them. And they expressed no surprise at anything I told them. Just nodded occasionally, in a grave way, as if their worst fears were being confirmed. Just once, Mr Shaftesbury muttered something to Mr Maidment that sounded like Latin. '*Malleus malificorum*', I think. Mr Maidment gave him a look that silenced him immediately.

They heard me out to the finish. At the same time, they seemed to regard Hermione as a creature of no importance, as if only men were worth listening to, however sinful they might be.

At the end, Mr Maidment said, 'Was it your impression that the seat of the creature was in the cellars?'

'Yes,' said Hermione. He gave her a look as if he was surprised she was there at all, and disgusted that she should dare to speak. When he had stared at her enough for his purpose, he returned his gaze to me. And asked me the question all over again.

I wanted to say, 'Why can't you take Hermione's word for it?' But all that came out was a weak. 'Yes'.

'Has the creature any force outside the house?'

'No,' I said. 'I don't think so. Only . . . through the mud from the Pond. Or the things we took out of the Pond.'

They all three nodded. 'A binding prayer,' said Mr Crombie, with a little flicker of excitement in his dark sombre eyes.

He got the same treatment as Mr Shaftesbury had got. This Maidment creature, did he think he was God?

'In the cellars, was there . . . stonework? Old stonework?'

I wanted to say, 'Ask Hermione, she was in front.' But it died on my lips. So I said, 'I caught a brief glimpse of some old rough stonework.'

'Have there been any instances of people snatched from their beds? Unexplained pools of blood or pieces of flesh in the open air?'

'Not that I've heard of. The only people we know have vanished have been those who lived in that house.'

He nodded, and seemed relieved. If such a face could show relief.

'So it holds. But for how long? If the house was to be demolished . . . the only solution is fire. Fire to the foundations. Fire beneath the foundations.'

The other two nodded. They got to their feet. They looked down at poor James, who tried to raise his eyes to them, like a beaten spaniel, in a way that made me sick.

'James will see to it. When you are ready, James, let us know. We will be there.'

'And then without a word, without a thank you or a nod, they left.

When the front door had closed, I exploded.

'Bloody nerve. Who the hell do they think they are?'

'They're the ones who understand,' said James. 'They're the ones who know what to do. What must be done.'

'Oh yes,' I said. 'They're very good at giving orders. Just burn that house down, James. You could get ten years in prison for that. But we'll come and watch, James. It's just that we don't want to get our own hands dirty.'

'You don't understand, Mr Morgan. I know its been bad for you, but if that thing broke out of the binding prayer the monks must have put on it . . .'

'How do *they* know the monks put a binding prayer on it?'

James looked at me long. 'I'll only ask you one thing, Mr Morgan. Would you ever set foot in that house again?'

I collapsed like a house of cards.

'But as to how I do it,' said James grimly. 'Just a fire won't do, you see. Not ordinary fire . . . they'd just redevelop the site and it could start all over again.

And if the excavations loosen the binding prayer . . . then . . .'

Hermione stirred in the corner. She said, almost dreamily, 'You would need something like the Greek fire the Byzantines used. Something that would creep and drip and cling and go on burning . . .'

I said, 'You mean like napalm? How the hell would *we* get napalm? Ring up the USAF at Mildenhall and ask them if they've got any second-hand napalm going cheap?'

'The stuff they made Greek fire with is quite common – still in industrial use. Burning pitch . . . phosphorous . . .'

'How do we get that?' asked James.

'Mossy might have contacts . . .' said Hermione.

'And who's going to pay Mossy?'

'Stop being so trivial and childish, Morgan . . .'

'And how do we get it inside? It's not going to just sit there and let us . . .'

'We'll just have to work it out, Morgan. Won't we?'

'Tomorrow night,' said Mossy down the phone. 'I'm sorry, but my bloke says it'll be ten thousand quid, Mr Morgan. Five thousand for the Landrover – the number-plates will slip off easily, and the engine and chassis numbers will be filed off. It won't be traceable. And he's shown me how to use the electronic timer. The Semtex cost a bit – it's getting very dodgy, Semtex, thanks to our friends across the Irish Sea.'

'Ten thousand quid?' I squealed.

'That's delivered to the site at a time of your choice. He's taking the risks. And he wants cash – ten and twenties, used notes. Right?'

'Right,' I said wearily. Anything to get out of this hideous fairyland. Anything to get back to bodging up antiques and cheating the good old British public again.

CHAPTER FOURTEEN

hy did everything go wrong that night? Was it just that we hadn't planned properly, hadn't reconnoitred thoroughly enough, not wanting to go near the place till it was time? Or was the creature reaching out to us, through the very flecks of mud engrained in our skin?

We crept into that accursed garden in good enough time; too early, perhaps, through nervousness: having left the cars parked not too far away for a quick get-away. Hermione, me, Mossy, James. We crept round the back of the house, and shone discreet torches on the great French window that was the only possible way in. It was as we remembered it: plenty of space to admit a Landrover, provided it smashed its way in through two slender carved columns of stone that looked like the grey leg-bones of a giant.

But we had forgotten the steep two-foot step leading up to the window. Which even a Landrover in bottom gear might find impossible to climb.

We stood, utterly dismayed, until Mossy said. 'We'll have to build a ramp.'

'With what?' My heart was in my boots.

His torch flicked round. 'Plenty of stones in the old rockery. Branches. And the suitcases in the outhouse. Some of them look solid enough.'

So we slaved, sweated in the warm night. The

suitcases, pulled into the open air, looked like the pathetic possessions that doomed Jews left, at the entrances to the death-camps. But I felt a certain grim irony in the fact that the dead too were having their revenge.

We finished the ramp at five to midnight. Stood back and waited.

'Here he comes,' said Mossy. Far off, up Belvoir Road, the rattle of the Landrover's old diesel engine rose clear of the sound of background traffic, which in London never stops all night.

'Got the money ready, Mr Morgan?' whispered Mossy. 'He'll want to get away quick, once he's delivered. He's the nervous sort. And it *is* the right amount, isn't it? It doesn't do to short-change that lot – you could get kneecapped.'

'Counted four times, Mossy.'

'Good.' He breathed a deep sigh of relief.

The Landrover hesitated outside the gate, then doused its lights and came silently bumping down the side of the house. The hand-brake went on. A little man got out, handed Mossy the keys, and held out his hand for the briefcase of money. My hard-earned savings were going God knew where, to serve God knew what cause. I badly wanted to see the face of the man I was giving it to. All I could see was a white ferret nose, sticking out between a turned-up collar and a pulled-down cap.

But he felt my eyes on him. Turned and looked at me very hard, as if trying to memorize my face, as if to say, well, you wanted to see one of us, and now you've seen one of us. The eyes glinted like the eyes of a rat, caught in the torch-beam. Only the eyes of a rat that was very sure of itself; a rat that knew it could bite and kill. I dearly wished I hadn't looked at him; I dearly wished he hadn't seen my face . . .

Then he was gone, taking his number-plates with him. We looked inside the Landrover. It was an old one: long wheelbase, hard top. All the stuff was there, the yellow chemical drums, the glass carboys of phosphorous in their metal baskets. And the small glowing figures on the electronic timer by the rear door. It reminded me of the black boxes that Ross and Makepeace still made . . .

'Better get moving,' said Mossy. 'He's set it. Ten minutes.'

He got into the driver's seat, restarted the engine, fiddled with the levers of the triple gearbox . . .

'She lined up right?'

We whispered soft instructions as he backed and turned the Landrover, lining it up with the French window.

'OK, now?'

He had leapt from the driver's seat, before the Landrover began moving. It edged so slowly up to the ramp, in its very bottom gear. Began to climb. The front bumper touched the stone pillars. The pillars began to grate and creak. In one second, this purely mechanical creature, that knew nothing of the things of the spirit, that was impervious to both good and evil, would have entered the body of its host, like a poison pill . . .

And then everything flew apart. With a crash and a crunch and a cascade of personal belongings, the ramp gave way. I saw, with despairing eyes, babies' bootees spilling on to the old gravel. The Landrover humped up and fell, and humped up again, as it tried to climb the obstacle and failed. There was a whining within it, a smell of burning. The clutch was starting to burn out, as the sagging right front wheel turned slowly, pointlessly . . .

I was ready to run. I saw it all, the whole disaster. The bomb would go off, outside the house. The phosphorous would spray everywhere, on the house walls, on the trees, on us . . . we would die, horribly. And the creature inside would live. And if the house did burn, it would only burn to the cellars, and be demolished, and the binding prayer would be broken and . . .

Somebody knocked me aside, so I fell flat on my face. I saw a figure scrambling into the driver's seat; heard the Landrover go into reverse, saw it roll back down among the trees.

And then the gears crashed again, and the engine roared like a wild beast, and the Landrover came back towards me at a terrible pace. I just wriggled aside in time, and it flew up the remains of the ramp and crashed into the stonework, and stopped dead.

Then again it reversed, steam pouring from its fractured radiator, and the gears crunched again, and now, screaming with the noise of tortured metal, its bonnet-lid forced vertical by the collision, its tyres screeching and giving off black smoke, it plunged at the window again.

There was a great tinkling of glass; the stone pillars bent inwards and snapped, and, with the heavy-treaded rear tyres still scrabbling and spewing massacred personal possessions, picture-frames and shoes and even a gaudy china vase, the Landrover lifted itself over the sill like a great weary beast, and bumped across the floor inside.

Until the floor gave way with a great splintering of

wood, and the vehicle crashed down into the cellars and out of sight.

And, as if to seal its fate, the wall of the house, weakened by the loss of the pillars, cracked and crashed down, filling the air with fine white powder.

Inside, the engine howled and died, and there was a great silence.

I heard, somewhere in the billowing dust, Mossy yelling, 'Who was it? Who was it?'

Somehow I knew utterly, fatally, that it had been Hermione.

Until she called out weakly from further down the garden.

'That bloke of yours,' shouted Mossy. 'I don't know his name.'

James. James, entombed, alone with the beast.

In fear and trembling we climbed up the rubble and peered through the vast hole where the wall should be. Small stuff – single bricks, and slates – were raining down from the roof above.

'James,' we shouted. 'James.'

It was when we had quite lost hope that we heard the voice; a strong voice, a singing voice, from out of the depths:

'Oh, my God, make them like a wheel
As the stubble before the wind
As the fire burneth a wood
And as the flame setteth the mountains on fire . . .'

'It's him,' whispered Hermione. 'It's James. He must be trapped in the driver's seat. C'mon, we must get him out.'

She started down; but Mossy grabbed her. 'Not time,' he shouted. 'Fifty seconds to go.'

So, like cowards, we left him, and ran, scrambled, to save ourselves.

And not a moment too soon. From the depths of the earth came a short sharp crump and a small red flash, and a tremble under our feet. A shower of white stuff sailed out of the hole the Landrover had made, and splattered down among the trees. The smell was chemical, and hurt our noses.

And then, it was as if it was instant autumn. A yellow flame blossomed among the heavy ornamental foliage overhead. And another, and another. Now there were dozens. And the flames began to drip downwards. Whole trees catching fire. A piece fell at my feet, and the long-dead damp leaves began to smoke.

'Get the hell out,' shouted Mossy. 'There's nothing we can do here.'

But we saw it all, from the front gate, through the front windows of Abbeywalk. The leaping red flames inside, that slowly turned into a molten heart of fire, and rolled and dripped among the fallen masonry within.

And then, incredibly, we heard the voice again, still singing:

'A fire goeth before him
And burneth up his enemies roundabout
His lightnings enlightened the world
The hills melted like wax in the presence of the Lord.'

'That's from higher up,' shouted Hermione. 'He's escaped. He's on the first floor. I could swear it.'

'You can't tell that,' shouted Mossy. You could hardly hear his voice, above the roar of the flames. 'He could be anywhere.'

But, as if in answer, we saw a human figure, gesturing, at a first-floor window. James. Blackened. But James.

'Jump!' we shouted. 'Break the glass. Jump!'

But he paid no heed to us.

'It's got hold of him,' said Hermione bitterly. 'It's got hold of his mind, now, like it got hold of us.'

Now the window where James had stood was a mass of flame; the glass shattered and tinkled outwards.

And all around us, through the darkened London air, came the sound of sirens. Police, fire, ambulance. Too late.

A screech of brakes, a shower of gravel. Then Crittenden's voice at my shoulder. Sarcastic as ever.

'What're you up to now, Mr Morgan? Arson? For the insurance?'

I opened my mouth, but I never had time to think what to say.

For I heard another sound now, another voice. A voice so huge it deafened. A voice of garbled syllables, in a dreadful language I had no wish to understand. A voice that must have been heard all over London. In St John's Wood, and Chalk Farm, and even on the Heath. A voice of pure rage, that shouted and was silent.

'My God,' said Crittenden. 'What's that?' Even in the ruddy light of the fire, his face was white and chalky.

'That's what killed Margie Duff,' I said. 'And Tony Tanner.'

The dreadful yell came again. And there was more than rage in it now. There was agony and despair.

'It knows it's going to die,' whispered Hermione.

And so we listened in silence – police, firemen, even ambulance men – to those gigantic death-yells. Almost, it invited pity. It is a fearful thing for any creature to die in agony. And yet, till the end, it repelled pity. It was a long time in dying, for it must have been a gigantic thing.

By the time it had melted into silence, the whole of Abbeywalk was on fire. A dancing red showed in every window. Only the roof was still black, and that was showing forth wisps of smoke and steam from every crack, a grey wool that writhed round the pinnacles and gargoyles.

It was then that we saw him. James. Clinging to a pinnacle, above a second-floor gable. And still singing, though his voice was hoarse with smoke, and half-choked with coughing.

'Let burning coals fall upon them,
Let them be cast into the fire,
Into the deep pits . . . that they . . . rise not up again.'

And at the same moment, I saw the top of a monkey-puzzle tree in the front garden, rising to within a few feet of where he crouched.

And something made me shout, 'Jump, you silly sod.'

The death of the creature must somehow have released him. He heard me. He turned and looked at me, as a normal human being might. Now, everybody was shouting 'Jump', as the first section of roof, at his back, caved in, leaving a red gaping mouth like a furnace.

Whether sense came back to him then, or whether his holy work was done, or whether even a madman fears the fire, I shall never know.

He leapt. He reached the thin tip of the monkey-puzzle tree and embraced it. Under his weight, it began to bend outwards; more and more. Just when it should have snapped, it collided with another, smaller tree. Now both trees were bending outwards. I heard and saw the first trunk snap. The second one bent more quickly. And then James was catapulted off into the centre of a mass of rhododendrons and, inside it, we heard him crash to the ground. And then we were all running, and burrowing into those bushes like mad.

I was the first to reach him, to hear his high panting. His two strong hands grasped me, and with their strength, I knew he was going to live.

'They ... that wait ... upon the Lord ... shall renew their strength,' he said.

'I don't call *that* mounting up on wings as eagles,' I said. I was that glad to have him back.

Then the ambulance men were moving in, with their calm, slow cleverness.

'I suppose I ought to charge you with arson,' said Sergeant Crittenden, taking me aside. 'But I heard that ... thing. And I reckon you did Wheatstone a public service. Now I don't know what the hell to do. I mean, what we going to find in there? What's the fire brigade goin' to find?' He nodded to where a few firemen were playing their hoses to contain what was now just a deep pit full of glowing red ash.

'A burnt-out Landrover,' I said. 'I doubt you'll find much else. I can't see you getting a giant misshapen skull or thigh-bone. Not at that temperature.'

'Pity,' he said thinly. 'A gigantic misshapen skull is just what our nick needs.'

How could we have laughed? But they tell me people laughed in the Blitz, when they'd just been blown twenty yards by a bomb. We were none of us quite sane that night.

'They will also find traces of phosphorous, all over these burnt trees. And pitch, and Semtex . . .'

'Oh shit,' said Crittenden. 'Bought the stuff off the IRA, did you?'

'Don't know. He didn't leave a calling-card.'

'Mebbe they'll blame it on the owner of the premises. Mebbe they'll think *he* was after the insurance.'

'It couldn't happen to a nastier guy,' I said. 'In my opinion, he knew perfectly well what was going on. Just went off to sunny climes, and let the thing get on with it.'

'What worries me is the lack of evidence,' said Crittenden. 'Nothing to show.'

'Oh, I've got something that will interest your forensic scientists,' I said. 'In an outhouse at my antique shop. A large model steam-yacht. With contents. And they're welcome to it.'

We flung the doors wide. The smell was so appalling we had to wait half an hour for it to clear. And then it still hung around. I have never used that outhouse again from that day to this.

Wearing the rubber gloves we use for stripping

paintwork I gingerly lifted the hatch of the forward saloon of the *Circe* and craned forward, holding my nose.

Crittenden looked long. 'What was I supposed to see?'

'Three tiny skeletons, about a foot long. One bigger than the others.'

'Get away! And now somebody's nicked them?'

I poked at the top of three tiny white skulls, like pieces of eggshell, that still protruded from the stinking mass of ooze. But they dissolved under my hand. Like all the rest of the little skeletons.

'Rotted away, I suppose,' said Hermione. 'On contact with the air.'

'I'll be in touch,' said Crittenden, and backed out and went off to his car, holding a white hanky to his nose and blowing vigorously, to get the smell out of it.

For a last time, Hermione and I stood on the shores of the Wheatstone Pond. The old crumbling Tarmac had been mashed by the tyres of great lorries. Only odd lumps of the sandstone kerbing stuck up still, like an old man's rotting teeth. The smell of brick-dust, old sooty London brick-dust, drifted to our nostrils on the breeze, as the line of three JCBs did their gnawing, trampling work, far out on what had once been water. The trees on the ornamental island were mere white stumps. Soon, under those great arcing jaws, they too would be gone. Next week, the earth would be brought in. Soon, grass-seed would be sown. Kids would romp, and mums push prams.

'I just hope all that foul ooze . . . is all *gone*,' said Hermione.

'Did you notice . . . the local crime figures jumped, just after they'd stopped pumping? A lot of the ooze must have blown round as dust, I suppose. I nearly gave up breathing for a bit, till the smell finally went.'

'You wonder where the stuff's gone now . . . bet its still upsetting somebody somewhere.'

'In smaller and smaller doses . . . adding to the misery of the world.'

'I suppose we shall never know exactly what happened to J. Montague Wheeler . . .'

'I reckon it was like Faust and Mephistopheles. Mephistopheles offered Faust all worldly power, in exchange for his soul. Riches, women, all his wildest dreams. Well, I reckon J. Montague Wheeler's wildest dream was to get inside his dinky model yacht, and sail it round the Wheatstone Pond. In the middle of the night. And it went horribly, horribly wrong. Maybe Mephistopheles got tired of J. Montague Wheeler and his sons. Maybe they were getting crazier and crazier. Maybe they were planning to sail the *Circe* in broad daylight, to the amazement of their friends in the Wheatstone Yachting Club, Steam Section. Maybe they were threatening to blow Mephistopheles' cover with their little pranks. Maybe Mephistopheles couldn't afford J. Montague Wheeler any more . . . or maybe his time was just up.'

Hermione shuddered. 'I used to have the same dream as a child. To become small, so I could sail on my little model yacht.'

'So did I. It's a dream most kids have.'

'And all the other people, and all their dreams. I wonder what dream the Belgian girl had, or Tony Tanner, or Margie Duff? . . .'

'We shall never know. We can only guess. Anyway, I'm sticking to faking antiques in future.'

'And I've got an exhibition of model boats to prepare for the City Toy Museum. I don't know how I'm going to face it.' She hugged herself with both arms. 'I know one thing; *Circe* is not going to be part of it. You can have her.'

'Mr Makepeace can have her.'

'Would you sell it to him, knowing what you know now?'

'Once she's scrubbed spotless, what his mind doesn't know his heart won't grieve ... it wasn't the boat's fault. She's a lovely bit of British craftsmanship ...'

'You'll never change, Morgan, will you?'

'Neither will you.'

And on that we parted. How can you fall in love with someone who knows you too well?

But we still dine out on the anniversary. Which is how I know what happened to the bloke who owned Abbeywalk. Hermione told me. He lost his grip on the stock exchange. The late 1987 crisis finished him, and he jumped out of a high window in San Francisco. It seems your sins do find you out in the end.

Well, your big ones, anyway.